I
PREFER
GIRLS

A NOVEL BY

JESSIE
DUMONT

BLACKBIRD BOOKS
NEW YORK • LOS ANGELES

A Blackbird Classic, May 2013

Cover painting by Robert Maguire

Manufactured in the United States of America.

The events and characters depicted in this book are fictional.

Cataloging-in-Publication Data

Dumont, Jessie.
I prefer girls / Jessie Dumont.
p. cm.
1. Lesbians—Fiction. 2. Heterosexual women—Fiction
3. Lesbians—Interpersonal relations—Fiction. 4. Triangles
(Interpersonal relations)—Fiction. 5. Men—Relations with
lesbians—Fiction. I. Title.
PS3554.U46 I6 2013 813'.54—dc22 2013941120

Blackbird Books
www.bbirdbooks.com
email us at editor@bbirdbooks.com

ISBN 978-1-61053-016-3

First Blackbird Edition

10 9 8 7 6 5 4 3 2 1

I
PREFER
GIRLS

1.

GREENWICH VILLAGE IS ALL RIGHT TO LIVE IN, but I wouldn't want to visit it.

It's especially bad on Saturday nights. That's when all the goddamned tourists come pouring up out of the subways, like lemmings or something, and just swarm all over the streets. I swear to God, it's enough to make you sick—the way they stand around gawking at the coffee shops, staring at the natives, laughing and pointing and making bigger fools out of themselves than they already are.

I wonder if any of them know just how much we hate them.

That's why I wouldn't want to be a visitor in the Village.

It must be a hell of a thing to be hated like that.

But as a place to live, the Village is just fine. You've probably heard that the area is filled with loonies. Well, that's the truth. I guess there are more crazy people per square foot in the Village than you'll find almost anywhere else in the world.

You've probably also heard that loonies are hard to get along with, and that's a lie. A nut usually isn't nearly as critical of his fellow man as a so-called normal person can be. A nut has his own ideas about life, and he knows that he can conduct his affairs his own way only if people leave him alone. And one of the best methods of keeping people's noses out of your business is to keep *your nose* out of *theirs.*

Live and let live: that's the motto in the Village. And it works out very well.

Take it from a gal who knows.

Who am I?

Well, that's a good question, and I certainly wish I had a good answer for it. It would be nice if I could put myself in a nutshell for you, sum up everything I've been and everything I've done in a nice neat little package so you could label me.

But, unfortunately, people aren't as simple as that—at least, not in the Village they aren't. Maybe the folks in Brooklyn or Queens or Flushing are different—I don't know—but trying to describe a Villager in a word is like trying to put together a dictionary with only one definition in it.

You can start with sex, I suppose—on second thought, better make that word *gender,* just to avoid confusion. Physically, just about everyone in the Village is either a man or a woman, even if it is sometimes a little hard to tell.

I'm a woman.

Then there are background and education and family—things like that. No two people are alike in that respect, especially in the Village, so I can speak only for myself.

My parents named me Penelope, which is one of the ugliest names under the sun as far as I'm concerned. It's so damned ugly, in fact, that I never use it; I just call myself Penny.

Penny Stewart.

I was born and raised right here in New York, in the Bronx to be exact. I don't remember a hell of a lot about my childhood, probably because most of it was so bloody dull. To tell you the truth, I can't even remember my parents clearly anymore.

When I try to picture my mother, all I can see is a fat old woman, sitting in a chair and crying. I don't recall what she was crying about.

And when I think of my father, I see only a hand with a strap in it. My father used to hit me quite a bit, and I guess it serves him right that I don't remember anything about him but the strap.

A crying woman, and a hand with a strap—that was Mom and Dad.

Why did I get hit so much? I don't recall that, either. I guess I must have misbehaved a lot when I was a girl, or at least done things which my mother and father considered misbehavior. I used to get into a lot of fights in my old neighborhood; I used to take pot shots at the local cats and dogs with this air rifle I had; and there was a snot-nosed little crud down the block a couple of years younger than me— Seymour, his name was—who I used to beat up every chance I got.

Perhaps those were the things which upset my parents so, although all the other kids in the neighborhood did the same, and I don't recollect ever hearing about any of them getting strapped by their fathers.

Come to think of it, practically all my friends were boys. I enjoyed myself more with boys than with girls. I preferred to play ball, climb trees, bloody somebody's nose, and I wanted no part of things like dolls, playing house, dressing up.

I wasn't a very feminine little girl, and maybe that's what my parents didn't like about me.

I got through grammar school by the skin of my teeth. I was always a lousy student—not because I was stupid or anything, but because I just didn't give a damn. I thought the idea of learning all about things was great, but I didn't care for having knowledge stuffed down my throat whether I was in the mood for it or not. School to me was like a prison—do this, do that, do it even if you don't want to, do it because we tell you to do it.

The hell with that.

Although the memory is hazy, I think I got in trouble a few times because of school. I know none of the teachers cared for me very much because I wouldn't pay attention to the work. I preferred to kid around, pass notes, throw spitballs, that sort of thing.

Once I remember one of the girls in my class told me I was ugly. I got her in the coatroom after class and I would have whaled the goddamn tar out of her if our teacher hadn't come back to get something and found us there. That must have been one of the times my father took the strap to me. But I can't be sure.

I didn't change very much when I got into high school. My marks stayed at a barely passing level, which infuriated both my parents and my teachers who were forever taking me aside and telling me that I wasn't doing my best work, wasn't living up to my potential. I didn't give a damn about my potential, or them, either; and I told them so, right to their faces. I wanted to do things my own way and in my own time, and anybody who thought different could just drop dead for all I cared. That must have made trouble for me, too; but if it did, I don't remember it.

High school presented another problem which had nothing to do with my work. Our school was co-educational and was always throwing dances and parties and garbage like that. There was about an equal number of boys and girls in the school, and the people in charge of these stupid get-togethers were never satisfied until they had paired every-body off with everybody else, boy-girl, boy-girl, all neat and orderly in a row, like marching convicts.

I wouldn't have any part of that. Going to school from nine to three was bad enough, but hanging around after-wards for some kind of dull party was out of the question. I wasn't interested in dating boys. If I went anywhere with a boy, it would be to raise some hell, not dance and drink punch in the school gymnasium.

The business of dating and going out with boys grew to be a real pain in the neck before I finally managed to gradu-ate from high school. God knows I tried to make my attitude plain enough, but nobody would ever take me seriously, es-pecially not the boys in my class. No matter how many times I told them to go jump, they'd keep coming back and sniff-ing around, fighting for a chance to date me.

That's because I was pretty.

I know I'm not supposed to blow my own horn, but the hell with that. I was a good-looking young girl; all I had to do was look in the mirror to see the truth of it.

The rough and tumble way I'd played around during my early years had hardened my body, but not so much that I didn't eventually develop all the curves a girl should have. My chest, which had been flat and hard as a boy's, started to fill out when I graduated from grammar school, and by the time I was through my first year of high school I had a set of breasts that were the envy of all the girls in class. My muscle-tone was good, and that made my breasts ride high and wide on my chest; in fact, they stood up so well all by themselves that I seldom even bothered to wear a bra.

The rest of my body was the same—hard, strong, but very female. I used to catch the boys looking at my legs and got a big kick out of the sloppy expressions they wore on their faces when they thought I wasn't watching them. I'm sure they were all just dying to get their hands on me and feel everything I had, the way boys always did on dates according to the stories I'd heard. But not a one of them ever got the chance. They could dream all they wanted, but they weren't going to get anything from me.

So I got out of high school, as I had out of grammar school, by the skin of my teeth.

And then came the big argument.

My stupid parents wanted me to go to college, which would mean more studying, more discipline, more of everything I hated so much. I wanted to go out and get a job and start leading my own life, without any help or interference from anybody. The difference of opinion at my house made for open warfare, and before that argument was settled I think my father took the strap to me a couple of times, although I don't remember for certain.

Anyway, they won. I had to abandon my dream of independence and start going to yet another goddamn school. It was no better than grammar or high school had been, and in one way it was worse. The fellows I came in contact with were older and more demanding, and they kept after me for dates night and day. I was, if you don't mind my saying so, developing into a knockout, but my ideas about boys hadn't changed at all. Now that I was too old to climb trees or break windows or kill cats with a boy, I couldn't think of a single reason to have anything to do with him.

This problem was complicated by the fact that most of the girls at that school let the boys have sex with them. I don't know if all colleges are like that, but there was usually more going on at night around that campus than you'd find in one of those wide-open Texas towns you read about in the newspapers. The girls seemed to consider it some kind of goddamned privilege to spread it out for the boys, which was a thing I didn't understand at all.

Maybe it was fun for them. Who knows?

The college phase of my life lasted just a year. Then one day, without any warning, my mother and father were dead. It happened in an automobile accident; my father, who could be pretty stupid sometimes, misread a sign and turned south onto a northbound lane of the Southern State Parkway. He ran head-on into a Buick, killing both himself and Mother in a blaze of glory, as well as the guy in the Buick whose name I never did catch.

And all of a sudden, I was free.

No more folks, no more orders, no more college, no more doing anything I didn't want to do. Mother and Father were the only relatives I had in all the world, and with them gone, there wasn't a soul anywhere with the right to tell me what to do.

Let me tell you, it was a great feeling. But it was also just a little bit scary. Wanting to be independent, self-supporting, on my own was a fine thing to dream about, but suddenly being faced with the necessity of taking care of myself wasn't as pleasant a reality as I had expected.

It took me a little time to get used to the notion. Luckily, mother and father had left behind some insurance money— enough to pay for their funeral, settle all the bills and keep me alive for three months or so. As you have probably gathered, I didn't have any friends to speak of, so I spent most of my time at home thinking hard about my future.

And, after a while, I thought of the Village.

The young people at college had talked about Greenwich Village as if it were heaven. In the Village, they said, you could be or do anything you happened to want, and nobody would give a damn because they were all too busy doing the same things themselves. In the Village, life was completely up to the individual and, because most of the individuals were artists, writers, sculptors, poets and other assorted odd types, the general patterns of existence could be pretty unusual.

In the Village you could just be yourself, and if you didn't mind an occasional rat in a coffee shop or a queer living in the apartment next to yours, you would have it made.

I pondered everything I had heard about Greenwich Village, and the more I thought on it the better the idea seemed. So I gave up my parents' rented home, said goodbye without tears to the places of my youth and moved downtown.

All right—that's my background.

What's happened to me since that time I think of as foreground, because for all intents and purposes my life didn't start until I moved into the Village and met Marcella. Up to that point, I thought I'd had a fairly clear idea of what kind of person I was, but actually I had no idea at all. It took Marcella to show me just how worthless all the previous years of my life had been and how exciting the years to come could be.

Maybe I should thank Marcella for that, but thanking people is against my nature.

So we come now to the final question, the last thing you need to know in order to get a clear picture of me.

What am I?

Let me tell you about me and Marcella, and that question will answer itself.

Marcella Lewis Originals is a small, stylish dress shop on one of the narrow Village streets, sandwiched in between a used book store and a Greek restaurant. It's only a few steps from the subway, and so it was one of the first things I saw the day I arrived in the Village. There was a sign in Marcella's narrow display window which said: *Girl Wanted.*

I had planned to look for an apartment before going job hunting, but the little dress shop appealed to me. Without even taking the time to think about it, I went inside. Marcella looked the same as she does now—squarish, a bit heavy although not at all fat, with a serious face framed by straight black hair, and delicate thin-fingered hands. She's not bad-looking in her way, but she's anything but pretty, and she couldn't be more different from me if she had been designed to show me off. I'm a redhead, for one thing, and I already told you about my body. As pretty as I am, though, I always look just a little better beside Marcella, and I think that's what first attracted me to her.

I asked her about the job. She asked if I had any experience, and I lied to her that I had. The salary wasn't very good, but it would do for a start, and she surprised me by offering to share her apartment with me on a reasonable fifty-fifty basis. She had a living room, kitchen and bedroom in back of the shop. There was only one bed, but that didn't mean anything to me at the time.

Marcella seemed oddly happy to have me and closed up the shop for the day so we could move in my stuff. She took me out to dinner that evening and treated me so royally that you'd think I was doing her some tremendous favor by moving into her pad.

As it turned out, I was.

That night when we went to bed, Marcella made a pass at me.

It stopped me cold. I knew right away what she was driving at, but I couldn't understand her reasons for wanting it. Boys and girls had that sort of fun together, but *girls and girls*—I had never heard of such a thing.

Marcella—who was very patient, and still is—explained it to me. She told me a word which described the sort of person she was; she told me a little about her past, about a filthy experience in her childhood with some lunatic molester and how that had turned her against men forever. She told me how she'd worked and saved until she had enough to open her dress shop, how she'd made friends in the Village and how she'd gradually been introduced into the life she was leading.

She offered to do the same for me.

So I let her try.

It was my first taste of sex, and I just loved it. I loved the feeling of Marcella's clever hands all over my body, I went crazy under her kisses and caresses and, when the time came for the biggest kick of all, I was mindless enough to go all the way with Marcella and let her go all the way with me.

That happened almost six years ago.

I'm twenty-five now, and Marcella and I still live together. There's no question of my being an employee anymore. I work in the shop only occasionally, but Marcella pays my way anyhow. I work in her bedroom to make sure she gets value for her money.

Nothing very important happened to me in those five years. I had some sexual flings with a few other people besides Marcella. A couple of them were men, so I'm not a virgin anymore, if you were wondering about that. But in spite of those outside activities, I always came back to the same old thing, because I like it.

I'm a lesbian.

And that's the last important fact you need to know about me.

All things considered, life is pretty good. I don't have to work for my wages, I have plenty of free time to go looking for fun, and the Village is filled with people who think along the same lines I do so I never want for a new partner. I'm one of the best-looking lesbians around, and it's so damned easy to bowl the local girls over that it sometimes isn't any fun at all.

I can't tell you why Marcella puts up with this. Maybe she's in love with me, or something—she's ten years older than me and very sentimental, and I wouldn't put it past her.

The only reason I stick with her is because of the money. If and until I can find somebody as well-heeled and permissive as good old Marcella, I might as well stay where I am.

When you boil it all down, I have only one problem. That's the business of the blackouts. Every once in a while something happens to me and I pull a blank. These spells, or whatever they are, don't last very long, and they don't seem to do me any harm. They've been going on for quite some time—maybe even since I was a little girl, although I can't remember whether or not that's so.

Marcella's usually around when it happens, and she tells me it's nothing to worry about. And I suppose an occasional faint is a small enough price to pay for all the fun I'm having.

Remember what I said before about all the crazy people in Greenwich Village?

Well, I'm one of them.

Let the stupid tourists come and go, let them look at me and wonder about me and dream their hot little dreams about what I'd be like in bed, about whether I would lay down for them if the price was right. Let the fat-bellied men from the suburbs stare at my legs and my bottom and my breasts all they want.

They're never going to get a thing from me.

I prefer girls, and nothing will ever change that.

2.

IT WAS A TUESDAY EVENING.

I'd been working with Marcella all afternoon, hanging out some new stock, repacking some numbers that hadn't moved for return. The day's business had been slow, and it didn't surprise me at all when Marcella said she was going to close the shop early.

"I feel like going out," I said.

"Oh?" Marcella was bent over a deep carton. Her head bobbed up. "Where to, hon?"

"I don't know. Anywhere. Just out." I turned and started to head for the apartment in back.

Behind me, Marcella asked, "Like some company, hon?"

"No," I said. I swear I could almost feel her disappointment. I never bothered to mince words with Marcella. It wasn't necessary, for one thing—I imagine if I were to kick her down a flight of stairs she would probably forgive me— and, besides, I enjoyed sticking the needle into her. For a woman her age, and with all her experience, she certainly had a thin hide.

I went to the bedroom and laid out a crisp new dress. My closet was always filled with fresh clothing. Marcella let me choose what I liked from the new stock and never batted an eye when I picked out the most expensive numbers.

I stripped down to my skin and went into the bathroom for a shower. The water felt good, the soap felt even better, and I gave myself a thorough rubdown, filling my hands with suds and smearing them all over my breasts, my belly, my thighs. Being touched was something I always enjoyed, even when the hands were my own.

I rinsed myself off, wrapped a towel around me and started to leave the bathroom. But, as usual, the mirror stopped me.

I'm never able to resist a mirror, and this one was a honey. It was attached to the back of the bathroom door and ran from the top of it all the way to the floor. When I stood and looked at myself, all I could see behind me were the shower curtains, as if I were standing on a stage.

It was a great effect.

I examined myself carefully. My hair was a bit tousled, but I decided to leave it that way. I'm one of those girls who looks good even when her hair isn't too well combed. I wear it long, and when it hangs loose to my shoulders it gives me a wild look, like a comic book jungle queen or something.

The shower had taken off all my make-up, but I decided to leave that the way it was, too. It contributed to the nature-girl illusion.

The way I was standing, with nothing on except that towel, I really did look like some kind of jungle princess. The idea made me laugh. I thought about all the men in the world who would go crazy to see me like this. Quite often, I found myself tempted to show it to a man, show him everything I had, lead him on, then cover it up at the last minute and leave him with nothing. That would really be a laugh. I made a mental note to do it one of these days.

I stopped thinking about men and started thinking of girls.

I let the towel fall away from one breast.

It was round and smooth as a scoop of ice cream and shaped in a perfect teardrop. The tip was a circle about the size of a quarter, red and pebbled like a pale strawberry.

I don't know whether it was the touch of the air against me or my own thoughts which made it happen, but all of a sudden I noticed the tip of that exposed breast beginning to sculpt with excitement.

I dropped the towel a little further and saw that the same thing was happening to the other breast.

I dropped the towel all the way.

Looking at my naked body was one of the biggest pleasures I had. I'd seen plenty of other girls naked, and some of them were real beauties, but I'd never met one with half as good a figure as my own. I was egotistical about my physical development, but I had a right to be.

I lifted my arms above my head. The motion made my breasts draw up at a tip-tilted angle, tight and round and firm. I wriggled my hips a bit, the way strippers do, and watched the play of muscle all along my nude torso.

I wasn't a little girl anymore—no question about that—but my anatomy was as solid as it had ever been. I put my arms at my sides and gave a small jump. Nothing jiggled but my breasts, and they moved just enough.

Finally, I stuck out my tongue at my reflection, wrapped the towel around me again and went back into the bedroom.

Marcella was there waiting for me, sitting like a lump on the edge of the bed and smoking a cigarette. As I passed by her, I took the cigarette out of her hand.

"Penny?" she said. She sounded hurt.

"What?"

"Where will you be if I want to find you?"

"I don't know. Why would you want to find me?"

"Well, I might need you for something, hon."

I turned to face her and let the towel fall.

"Like what, Marcella?"

Her face went all slack, and it was really an effort to keep from laughing at her expression. To look at her, you'd think she had never seen my body before much less shared so many intimacies with me. I knew how to catch Marcella off-guard that way, and every time I did it I was struck with the resemblance between her lust-clogged expression and the faces of those cruddy men from the suburbs.

"What would you need me for, Marcella?" I asked.

"Nothing." Her eyes fell. "Put something on, hon. You'll catch cold."

"Not as long as I have you to keep me warm," I said. I went to the bureau and got out a bra and panties without looking to see what she thought of that remark. I carried them over to the bed and put them on within inches of her. Her hands were folded so tightly in her lap that all the blood was driven out of her knuckles; it was all she could do to keep her fingers off me.

It had been a warm day, so I didn't bother with a slip. I decided not to wear stockings either. My legs didn't need them. I pulled the new dress over *my* head and smoothed it into place. It was a pale tan jersey, with a square-cut neckline that showed off the first couple of inches of my cleavage. The hemline, according to the current style, rode a fraction of an inch above my knees.

I stuck my feet into a pair of tan high-heeled shoes and stepped out in front of Marcella.

"How do I look?"

She raised her eyes slowly. Her hands were still knotted in her lap. "Lovely," she said. "You look just lovely, hon."

I laughed. "I bet you say that to all the girls."

"There aren't any other girls, Penny. You know that."

I kept the smile pasted on my face. "Aren't there?" I asked.

"Penny? What time will you be home?"

I bent to one side until I could see myself in the bureau mirror and pushed at my hair. "I couldn't say. Depends where I go. If I find anything interesting, I might be gone for quite a while."

"Please, Penny," Marcella said.

I turned my most innocent face toward her. "Please *what*, Marcella?"

Her hands moved in her lap. "Forget it."

"Okay." I picked up my purse. "I already have."

As I started for the front of the place, Marcella called after me. "Shall I wait up for you, hon?"

"Do what you like," I said. "It could be a long wait."

She didn't say another word. Just for good measure, I slammed the door on my way out.

It was a beautiful evening. The sun had just gone behind the tops of the buildings, throwing the streets into cool shadow. Lights were coming on in all the windows, and people were beginning to drift into the street.

I turned my back on Marcella's dress shop and began walking.

On a week night, the Village can be a beautiful place. The store windows are filled with mad and wonderful things made by fag artists, and every time you pass a coffee shop you can smell the winey black aroma of an espresso machine going. Overhead, on the second and third floors, you can hear music playing from hi-fi rigs, or somebody with a guitar singing folk songs. Sometimes you can hear people fighting, and that's fun, too.

All in all, as long as there aren't any blasted tourists around, the Village is a marvelous neighborhood for a nice leisurely stroll.

In spite of the way I'd jabbed Marcella, I really didn't have any plans for the evening. I felt comfortable, pleased with myself and my life, and I wasn't out looking for anything. I supposed I'd walk for a while, then hit one of the coffee shops and wait around for someone I knew to show up. I was in the mood to relax, chat with an acquaintance and just spend a quiet evening away from Marcella.

I wasn't in the mood to sin at all.

But what a person wants and what fate decides to give her are often two completely different things.

I didn't know it, but something was going to happen that evening that would change my whole life.

Around nine o'clock, I got sick of walking and headed for a coffee shop. The one nearest me was also one of my favorites. It was called Pinocchio's for some screwball reason, and a fellow named Andrew ran it. I liked Andrew. He was queer as a thirteen-dollar bill and made no secret of the fact. And since I was the same way about my own personal twist, Andrew and I got along just fine.

Pinocchio's was a bit crowded for a Tuesday evening, and I knew the minute I walked in that Andrew would be too busy to talk to me. I spotted him in back, pouring boiling water into the top of the espresso machine, and waved. He grinned his usual swishy grin.

I looked around and discovered an empty table by the window. I wanted to sit where I could see the street in case someone I knew happened by. As I walked to the table, I noticed a couple of young men following me with their eyes. I didn't recognize them, but I knew damned well why they were looking at me. Just to make it worse for them, I sucked in a deep breath and drew myself up very straight, forcing my breasts tightly against the material of my dress.

I heard one of them make a hissing sound between his teeth.

I sat down with my back to them and lit a cigarette. I was almost hoping that one of the fellows would come over to my table and try to make a play. That happened to me fairly often, and I always got a big charge out of telling off the young punks, making them look like idiots. I was good at that.

I felt a footfall on the floor behind my chair and braced myself.

"Yes?" said a girl's voice.

A moment later, she had moved around to where I could see her.

The first thing I noticed about her was that she was new in Pinocchio's. I knew all the girls who worked for Andrew, and I'd never seen this one before.

The second thing I noticed was that she was beautiful.

She was wearing a wide black skirt, a heavy sweater and sandals. Her blond hair was pulled back into a pony-tail. Her face was clean of make-up, and she wasn't even wearing nail polish.

But none of that made the slightest difference.

Not even that hairy-looking sweater could disguise the sweet lines of her youthful bust, and in spite of the heavy skirt I could somehow tell that her hips and thighs were rounded and slender, just the way they ought to be. And her face . . .

She had a face like a little girl, pure and rosy and open, as if none of life's ugliness had ever penetrated into her mind. She didn't look stupid—she looked sheltered, untouched and completely virginal.

I sat there for a long moment simply staring at her, so surprised by her beauty that I couldn't even bring myself to speak.

"Yes, Miss?" she said. "May I help you?"

Her voice had a childish bell-like quality that positively sent chills up my spine.

"Yes," I said. "American coffee. Black."

"Of course." She scribbled it on a check. Her fingers were very long and slender. "Will there be anything else?"

"No. Not right now."

"All right." She smiled at me, and her smile was one of the most dazzling things I had ever seen. Then she turned and headed back toward the counter.

I watched her go, staring at the pretty flexing of her smooth calves, at the swaying of her trim buttocks, devouring her with my eyes the way those two young boys had done with me. I didn't take my eyes off her while she drew the coffee and returned down the length of the place to my table.

As she came closer, she seemed to notice my attention and her step faltered. I suppose the expression on my face must have puzzled her.

"Is everything all right, Miss?" she asked.

"Fine," I said.

"Oh." She set the coffee down carefully, then backed off a short distance. "If you want anything else," she said, "I'll be right back there by the counter."

"Thanks," I said. "Maybe I'll take you up on that."

Her smile this time didn't come so easily. She nodded and went back to her duties.

I sat and watched her mindlessly for what seemed like an hour. I kept discovering new and subtle beauties in the way she moved, the way she held herself, her apparent unaware-ness of just how lovely she was. I'd never seen a girl in my life before who combined such innocence with a body and face like that. The sight of it was intoxicating.

I was snapped out of my reverie suddenly by the touch of a hand on my shoulder. I looked up and saw one of the young men standing over me. The other one was still sitting at the table, leaning forward expectantly.

"Hi," he said brightly.

"Beat it," I said. "I don't want any."

"How do you know that? You don't even know what I'm selling yet." His voice had a phony richness to it, as if he had taken speech training.

"Are you an actor?" I asked.

His face brightened. "Yes, that's right."

"Then roll over and play dead."

"Oh, come on," he said, laughing. "What the hell do you want to be so independent for? I just came over to say hello."

"Good for you. Now say goodbye."

"You can do better than that," he said.

"I can do better than *you*, anyway. Now, cool it. Go back and play with your little friend over there."

The good-humored look finally faded from his face. "You've got a pretty nasty mouth, haven't you?"

"That's right," I said.

He put a hand on the table and leaned forward. "How is that?" he asked slyly. "How come you're such a bitch?"

I smiled. "Why, didn't you know, sonny? All us dykes are that way."

He blinked. His features went soft and rubbery, like Marcella's always did when I said something that really hurt her.

After a moment, he straightened up and crossed back to his table without another word.

I finished my coffee, grinning to myself between swallows. The evening was off to a promising start. I took one last drag on my cigarette, doused it in the bottom of the coffee cup, then headed toward the back to talk to Andrew.

3.

HER NAME WAS BERNICE TAYLOR.

According to Andrew, she lived uptown somewhere, along one of the cheaper stretches of Riverside Drive. She had turned up at Pinocchio's about a week ago looking for a job. She didn't have any experience as a waitress—in Andrew's opinion, and he was pretty good about such things, she didn't have any experience at all—but being a waitress in a coffee shop didn't require very much beyond the simple skills of writing checks, making change and carrying coffee without spilling any into the saucer.

"So I hired her," Andrew said, in his pale faggy voice. "Really, Penny, she was such a pretty little thing and seemed so anxious to work for me, I had no choice but to take her on."

"I don't blame you," I said.

He tilted his head to one side and began to lisp slightly the way he always did when he was thinking dirty. "I get the definite impression that little Bernice looks good to you, dear. Stop me if I'm wrong."

"Go to hell," I said, laughing. "You know you're right."

"That's one of the things I just love about you, dear. You can be such an animal when you see something you want. So ruthless . . ." He began to chuckle to himself.

"What's she like, Andrew?" I asked, cutting him off. "Have you met any of her friends?"

"If she has friends, dear, they never come around here. She lives alone. In fact, she told me she doesn't even have any family."

Bernice was at the opposite end of the place cleaning off a table. I watched her graceful movements and felt my hands begin to tremble a bit.

"I don't get it," I said. "What the hell is she doing working in Pinocchio's? She doesn't look the Village type at all."

"Why, that's really very simple," Andrew lisped. "I would have thought your keen discerning eye would have figured that out right away, dear."

"Figured what out?"

"She wants to be an actress."

Of course. As Andrew said, I should have seen that immediately. The Village was filled with aspiring young girls who longed for a career on the stage. The Village was also filled with playhouses of various kinds and with playwrights who had never quite made it. Some of the theaters made out better than others, and they even managed to draw business from the uptown tourist trade; in the past few years, these houses had formed into what was known as the Off-Broadway circuit. But most of the Village theatres were labors of love, sponsored by fat old matrons from Westchester who thought it was just too cute to finance a Greenwich Village experimental theatre and get laid by a bony young actor in the bargain.

These theatres drew hopeful young thespians by the subway-load. There were damned near as many of them wandering the streets on weekends as there were tourists. A confirmed Villager like myself could usually spot them immediately; the dreamy optimism in their eyes gave them away, as did the manner in which they wore their cruddy-looking sweaters and dungarees and sandals—not because such clothing was serviceable and comfortable, but because it was the required uniform for an actress seeking work in the Village.

"I'm getting stupid in my old age," I said to Andrew. "Has she had any luck?"

He shrugged elaborately. "Who has?"

"Uh-huh. Maybe I should give her some lessons."

"Oh, I'm sure she'd be very grateful for that. Experience is the raw material of the acting profession, after all, and lesbianism is very big in contemporary drama."

I showed him my teeth. "If you weren't such a fag, I'd belt you in the mouth."

"My dear," he said, grinning, "if you weren't such a strapping, handsome specimen, I'd *let* you."

I laughed. "Thanks for the information, Andrew. What time does she get off?"

He looked at his watch. "In a half-hour or so—at eleven o'clock."

"Does she usually go straight home do you know, or what?"

"I couldn't tell you, dear. Why don't you go find out for yourself?"

"I'll do that."

"Of course you will, dear," he said as I walked away from him. "Of course you will."

I gave Bernice another careful once-over on my way out. For a moment, I considered opening a conversation right there in Pinocchio's, but I decided it wouldn't be such a good idea. When I introduced myself to the girl, I wanted it to be in somewhat more cozy surroundings and not within sight of Andrew's twinkling and cynical eyes.

I went outside, leaned my butt against the fender of a car, lit a cigarette and waited. I caught sight of Bernice a few times through the front window of Pinocchio's, but mostly I saw her in my mind's eye, saw her not in the costume of a coffee shop waitress, but in the costume of a lesbian—in other words, nothing but her bare skin.

The vision was intoxicating.

It wasn't like me to do such a flip over a girl on my first meeting, and I worried a little about that. One of the reasons I prefer girls as sexual partners is because they're so easy to dominate if you know how. When a boy goes to bed with a girl, he wants to be in charge because he feels it's his masculine right, or some such foolishness. But when two girls make it together, they start off on an equal basis, and without differences in gender to complicate things the mastery of the situation goes to the one best equipped to handle it.

In all my affairs, that one had always been me.

But I had a strange feeling my relationship with Bernice, if I could get it off the ground, was going to be different. Something about her was really getting to me, and if I let myself be blinded by that special quality, whatever it was, I might find myself suddenly hitched to *her* wagon, rather than vice versa. It wasn't a very pleasant thought, but I wrote it up big and pasted it on a prominent spot inside my forehead where my mind's eye could see it.

Bernice was a toothsome little morsel, but no girl in the world was worth surrendering control for. Without domination, how would sex be any fun?

At five minutes to eleven, the two young men who had shown such an interest in me came out of Pinocchio's. They stopped by the door, lit cigarettes and talked for a while. Neither of them noticed me, and I paid no attention to them.

At eleven o'clock on the nose, Bernice came through the door.

I pushed myself away from the car and began to walk toward her. I hadn't gone three steps, however, when I saw one of the young fellows turn to look at her. He was the same little punk who had come over to my table.

I was close enough to hear him as he said, in that ersatz-mellow voice of his, "Well, *hello.* Going our way?"

Bernice seemed startled by the remark. She paused and looked at him. "Who are you?" she asked.

"I'm Mutt," said the fellow. "And he's Jeff. And who might you be?"

"I have to go now," she said. "Nice to meet you."

"Hey, wait a minute." He put a hand on her arm. "We're only getting started."

"Please," she said, pulling against his hand.

"Now, come on, little girl. All we're asking for is a chance to get acquainted. Is that so terrible?"

Bernice was beginning to look a bit frightened. "I have to go," she said again. "There's somebody I have to meet."

"Sure, sure. There were two people you had to meet—us." His hand left her arm and scooped around her waist.

I moved forward quickly.

"Hands off, punk. Let the girl go."

He stared at me, and his face went through several expressions in rapid order: surprise, annoyance, fear arid finally anger. "Well, well," he said tightly. "Look who's here—our pretty friend from Lesbos."

Fortunately, Bernice seemed too upset to catch the significance of that crack. I knew I would have to move fast if I didn't want this loud-mouthed young bum to spill my secret to Bernice. Of course she was going to find out I was a lesbian eventually, but I wanted that to happen in my own time and in my own way.

I took Bernice's hand in what I hoped was a comforting gesture. "Don't let these pansies bother you," I said. "Queers get like that sometimes."

The young fellow exploded. "Who're you calling a queer, you goddamn les—"

I belted him across the face with all the strength I had before he could get the word out.

And damn the silly bastard if he didn't ball up his fist, draw his arm back and aim a punch at me that would have taken off the top of my head. I let go of Bernice and braced myself, hoping I could ride with it enough to protect my face from damage. I set one foot firmly on the ground and cocked my other knee, waiting for an opening to give it to him where he lived.

He never threw that punch.

All at once, a hand came out of nowhere and detonated in the kid's face. It was really one hell of a blow, and the sound it made was as loud as the crack of a whip.

The boy spun away from the punch, blood spouting from his nostrils. The other fellow—his friend—lunged forward quickly, but he ran right into another of those magnificent punches. His head snapped around viciously and his eyes glazed, but he managed to stay on his feet long enough to get another shot, this time dead in the center of his belly.

He folded as neatly as a pair of trousers over a hanger. A second later, he toppled onto his side and lay there bubbling on the sidewalk.

The other fellow was sitting up. He passed the back of his hand under his nose, smearing blood all over his jaw. "All right," he said loudly. "That's enough, for God's sake. We didn't do any harm. You can't blame a guy for trying."

I noticed with satisfaction that all the speech-class depth had vanished from his voice.

The owner of those marvelous fists stepped forward. He was a big guy, with the tough raw-boned look you see on those tattooed men in TV cigarette commercials. He radiated maleness, but there was nothing self-conscious about it; he was all man, but he didn't look as if he had ever given any thought to the fact.

In a way, he was a lot like Bernice—a perfect specimen of his type without the ego to realize it.

"Get up," he said, in a voice that was legitimately deep and very angry. "Move your asses out of here."

The boy with the bloody nose scrambled up quickly and tried to get his friend on his feet. He was still bent double and was making a dry heaving sound in his throat. Somehow, the pair of them managed to stumble off down the street. They passed out of sight around the corner.

The big fellow turned to Bernice and touched her cheek gently. "Are you all right, sweetheart?"

"Oh, Mark," she said. Her voice broke, and she fell into his arms.

I stood there watching them like a statue in the park. I was still a bit numb from the trouble with those two kids, but it wasn't that which froze up my mind. It was the sight of Bernice, pretty little Bernice, the tasty plum I had thought would be mine, cuddled in the arms of a man, holding him tightly around the waist, her sweet body molded up against him full length, her lovely face buried against his chest . . .

Bernice—in the arms of a goddamned *man*.

It was too big a challenge for a person like me to ignore.

In that moment, what had been nothing but a lustful desire began to grow into an obsession.

4.

THE THREE OF US WENT TO A BAR NEARBY.

The big fellow settled us into a rear booth and wouldn't let me or Bernice say anything until he had ordered a round of drinks. He commanded us to take a healthy swallow, which was an order I didn't mind obeying at all.

Bernice choked a little on her drink. It logically fit her character that she was unused to hard liquor. I filed that fact away for future reference; it could, I thought, come in very handy.

The big guy reached across the table and took Bernice's hands as if he owned them. "What happened, sweetheart?"

"Oh, Mark," she said, and there was still a tremor in her voice, "it was terrible. These two boys—I was just leaving the restaurant to meet you, and they were waiting outside."

"Did you ever see them before?" he asked.

"Yes," she said. "They'd been in the place all evening. I waited on them. But they didn't say anything to me, never acted as if they were going to, make any trouble or anything. I don't understand it."

"They were wise guys," I said.

He looked at me. "Oh?"

"One of them came over to my table and tried for a pickup. I told him to go to hell. I guess that's what set them off and caused the trouble with Bernice. If it was, I'm sorry."

"It's not your fault there are punks like that roaming the streets," he said. "This is a trashy neighborhood." He turned back to Bernice. "I've told you that over and over again, sweetheart. Maybe now you'll believe me,"

"Don't be an idiot," I said to him. "A thing like that could happen anywhere."

He ignored me. "Did they hurt you, baby?" he asked Bernice.

"No," she said. She took a very deep breath. "I think they might have if this lady hadn't happened along." Bernice looked at me. "You were in the coffee shop this evening, too, weren't you?"

"That's right," I said. "You waited on me."

"I thought you left."

"I waited around outside," I said. "Felt like some fresh air. You know."

She smiled shallowly. "It's lucky for me you did."

The big man frowned. "I don't get it," he said. "What happened?"

"One of those awful boys tried to grab me," Bernice said. "He—he put his arm around me and said—"

"What did he say, baby?"

She seemed puzzled. "I don't really remember. Something dirty, I think . . . but I can't recall what it was."

Mentally, I breathed a sigh of relief. Bernice had heard the lesbian remarks, but apparently she hadn't understood them. Score one for my side.

"Anyway," Bernice continued, "I tried to get out of his grip, but he was too strong for me. And oh, Mark—I was so scared. I didn't know what he was going to do."

He nodded. "Uh-huh. Then what?"

"This lady here came out of thin air and told him to leave me alone. But he wouldn't." Bernice turned to me and smiled a smile that made me melt inside. "So she hit him."

"She did *what?*" He couldn't seem to believe his ears.

"She *did,*" Bernice said. "She gave him a real clout, right across the face."

"Well, I'll be damned," he said, laughing. "I didn't know that. I saw you struggling as I came up, but I didn't see any punches thrown."

"I had to do something," I said. "I was the only one around."

He stared at me as if he were really seeing me for the first time. His eyes scanned my face, then dipped to my breasts. His gaze was frank, and I could tell that he thought I was a beautiful woman. But somehow there was no sexual interest in his expression at all. I got the feeling that good-looking women were no novelty to him, and that at the moment he had eyes only for Bernice.

Score one for his side, curse him, and that made us even again.

"Well, thanks very much for your help," he said awkwardly.

"Think nothing of it," I said. "Glad to oblige."

"May I ask your name, Miss?"

"Sure. Penny Stewart. And you're . . . ?" I stuck out my hand.

"Mark Hughes." He shook hands with me. His palm was hard as rock, and I could feel the tremendous strength in him even in that light grip. "Do you live around here, Miss Stewart?"

"Call me Penny." I addressed that remark more to Bernice than to me. "Yes, I live just a few blocks away."

"Oh." He chewed his lip for a moment. "I'm sorry about that crack I made before."

"What crack?"

"That this was a trashy neighborhood. I didn't mean it the way it sounded. I was just mad, that's all."

He was genuinely embarrassed, and that put me one up on him. I made sure I didn't let go of the advantage.

"People think a lot of crazy things about the Village," I said. "Maybe we don't really get used to being insulted, but we learn to live with it."

He dropped my hand. "Sorry," he said again.

Bernice spoke to me for the first time. "Penny? What do you do?"

"I work in a dress shop," I said. "Marcella Lewis Originals, it's called. Drop around sometime, and I'll see to it that you're taken care of."

Out of the corner of my eye, I saw Mark stiffen slightly. I couldn't believe his male intuition was strong enough to catch the undertone of my remark, but I decided I had better start playing it a little more cool.

"How about you?" I asked Bernice.

"You know," she said. "I work in Pinocchio's."

"Oh, come on. A girl as pretty as you can't be planning a career as a waitress. You're good-looking enough to be an actress or something."

I had loaded my words with great care. I hit the bullseye.

"That's what I keep telling Mark," said Bernice. "But he thinks I'm crazy."

Mark formed his big hands around his glass. "I never said you were crazy, sweetheart. I only think that being an actress is no kind of life for a girl like you."

"And why not?" she asked. "What's so terrible about that sort of life? If I have talent, why shouldn't I go for a stage career?"

"You don't know yet whether you have any talent or not," said Mark.

Bernice looked at me in exasperation. "You hear that? Isn't it nice to have somebody on your side?"

"Come on, baby," Mark said quickly. "I wasn't trying to put you down. It's just that—well, so many people try to be actors, and so damned few of them make it. I worry sometimes that you'll get hurt."

"I was an actress for a couple of years myself," I lied. "And I never got hurt. In fact, I rather enjoyed it."

It did my heart good to see the way Bernice's face lit up. "*You* were on the stage?"

"Yes," I said. "Summer stock, upstate. Two whole seasons. It was great."

"Why didn't you keep on with it?" she asked.

I thought quickly. "My voice," I said. "I got a throat infection. And when I recovered, I couldn't really project anymore."

"Oh, how terrible for you." She put one of her warm little hands over mine. The contact made my flesh tingle.

"Your voice sounds all right to me," said Mark.

I looked at him levelly. "If you were in the balcony, it wouldn't."

"Can't anything be done for it?" Bernice asked.

"No," I said, faking a small sigh. I often wondered whether I should have been an actress after all; I'm so damned good at it. "But it's nothing to be sad about. I enjoy working in the shop, and every once in a while someone I knew from stock will turn up at one of the Village theatres." I paused; then, to make sure she got the point, I added: "It's nice to renew the old contacts."

Bernice was wearing a Christmas Morning face. "You actually *know* people in the Off-Broadway circuit?"

"A few," I said casually.

"Baby," said Mark, interrupting. "We should go now."

She shook her head quickly. "I want to talk to Penny."

"Sweetheart, it's almost midnight. I have to get up and go to work in the morning."

"Well, I don't," she said. "I don't start work until three o'clock in the afternoon."

"I want to take you home," he said. "For God's sake, that's why I came all the way down here to meet you—so I could see you home safely."

"I'm a big girl now, Mark. I'll be fine."

"Bernice," he said. "For the last time, will you—"

"Now, hold on a minute." Her voice rose. "I'm not in the mood for any ultimatums from you, Mark. You don't own me yet."

I didn't know what she meant by that, but I liked the sound of it.

"I never said I *owned* you, Bernice. Will you stop acting like a child and let me take you home?"

Her face grew cold. "You're not very nice to be with to-night," she said. "I think I'd rather go home by myself."

He sat hunched over his glass for a long moment, then got quickly to his feet. "All right, then," he said. "Have it your own way. I can't make you listen to me when you're like this."

"I intend to," she said, looking up at him. "I intend to have it *just* my own way. You'd better get used to that idea, Mark."

He stared at her, then turned his gaze toward me. There was anger in his eyes, but there was something else there, too, and I wondered again just how penetrating his intuition was. He wore the expression of a man who was worried about losing his girl, but I couldn't believe he had actually realized I was going to be his competition.

Our stares locked for only a few seconds. Then he turned and stamped out of the bar.

Bernice was looking down into her drink. I got the impression that the scene had upset her and tried to smooth it over before she had a change of heart.

"What was that all about?" I asked. "He talks as if he was your husband."

"We're engaged," she said quietly.

If that young punk in front of Pinocchio's had thrown his punch, I doubt if it would have hit me any harder than Bernice's words.

"Engaged!" I repeated stupidly. "That's nice. When's the big day?"

"We haven't really set a date yet." She held up her left hand. "That's why I don't have a ring."

"Oh. How come?"

She picked up her glass, took another sip of her drink
and began talking.

It seemed that Mark was working for an aircraft firm on
Long Island, not far from the town where she had been born
and raised. They had met about two years ago and had been
dating steadily ever since. The engagement wasn't formal
because neither of them were ready for marriage, but the
unspoken agreement was nevertheless mutual.

All her life, Bernice had nursed the dream of being an
actress. She had played in amateur groups on the Island, had
done some acting on a college radio station, but had never
come close enough to the big time to even smell it. In spite
of what she said to Mark, she wasn't at all sure she had talent; but, at the same time, she didn't want to give up the
dream until she tried it.

And then, all at once, things had changed. Bernice's
mother, her last surviving relative, died suddenly, leaving her
with no ties except Mark. For the first time in her life, she
was free to try for an acting career. Around the same time,
Mark heard of an opening in his firm's main plant, which
was in California. If he could swing the transfer, his salary
would be doubled, and he would be finally in a position to
marry and support Bernice.

Mark had three months in which to consider the transfer.
So he and Bernice had struck a bargain together. Although
he didn't approve of Bernice becoming an actress, he agreed
reluctantly that she was entitled to a try at it. Bernice pro-
posed that she get an apartment of her own somewhere in
New York City, find a job in the Village and see if she could
get an acting career underway. She admitted she didn't have

any real hope of succeeding, but she couldn't let the opportunity pass her by without at least making a stab at it.

So that was their deal. Bernice had three months to make good. If, in that time, she struck pay dirt, Mark would withdraw his objections and let her do what she wanted with her life. If, however, she fell on her face, as he was so certain she would, Bernice had promised him she would give up the idea forever and go to California to be his wife.

She ran through this story rapidly, and I could tell from the sound of her voice that the conflict between her dreams and her boyfriend was a pretty strong one. If I were going to get anywhere at all with her, it would only be through kid-glove handling.

"Do you love him?" I asked.

"Yes," she said. "Except when he's like he was tonight. He can be so damned pig-headed . . ."

"Well, men are like that."

She nodded. "That's a fact."

"Have you gotten anywhere?"

"Not yet," she said. "Of course, I've only been working in the Village for a week, and that's not long enough to get to know anybody. But I keep my eyes open for an opportunity. A lot of theatre people come into Pinocchio's, or so I'm told."

I wondered who was responsible for such an outrageous lie, but I didn't let my thoughts show on my face. "So you've only used up one week," I said. "That leaves you two months and three weeks to go, or thereabouts. Cheer up, Bernice. Something will happen yet. I can feel it in my bones."

Bernice looked at me intensely. "Maybe something already has," she said.

I tried to stay calm. I was used to good luck, but this was too beautiful to believe. "How do you mean?" I asked.

"Well, you said before that you know some theatre people . . ." She let the sentence trail off, as if embarrassed to come right out and ask me for a connection with those mythical theatre people of mine.

"Hey," I said, putting my hand on her arm. "That's right. Why the hell didn't I think of that?"

"Please, Penny," she said hurriedly. "I don't want you to get the impression that I'm digging for anything."

"Don't be silly, Bernice. It's no problem for me to introduce you to a few people. And if I can be instrumental in helping you along—well, fine. There's nothing I would like better."

I squeezed her upper arm chummily and felt the sudden soft pressure of a breast against the backs of my fingers. The contact made my stomach flop over, but Bernice didn't seem to notice it at all.

"Would you do that?" she asked, her eyes bright. "Would you *really* do that for me?"

"Sure. Why not?"

"I don't know." She dropped her eyes. "I'm not used to having people help me. Everybody I know tells me I'm crazy to want to be an actress."

"There's nothing crazy about it," I said gently. "People don't realize that actors and actresses are just human beings, not some kind of creatures from Mars. All anyone needs to be a performer are looks, poise and luck. And you have all of those."

"What about talent?" she asked.

"That's something you acquire," I said. "Contrary to what you've heard, people aren't born with talent. They learn it."

"Could you . . ." Once again, she couldn't push the request out.

"Would I teach you? Is that what you're asking?"

"I'm being very selfish," she said bleakly. "After all, I hardly know you."

I smiled. "I feel as if I know you pretty well, Bernice."

"Do you?"

"Yes. In fact, I wouldn't be at all surprised if we became very close friends."

"I'd like that," she breathed, and I swear to God there were stars in her eyes as she said it.

"Good," I said, struggling to keep my voice even. "It's a deal, then. We'll be friends, you and I—and I'll teach you everything you need to know."

Her smile was glowing with innocent delight, and I damned near had a heart attack when she cuddled her breast against the back of my hand.

It took all the self-control I had not to try anything on Bernice that evening. But the voice of caution was stronger than my glands, luckily, and I succeeded in holding off.

We stayed in the bar and talked until about two in the morning. Bernice asked me one question after another, and I strained my brain making up lies for her. After a while, the twin efforts of holding myself in check and concocting stories about my acting career became too much for me, and I suggested we break it up. Bernice would probably have talked to me all night if I'd let her.

I walked her to the subway. As she went down the stairs, she stopped and looked back at me. "You're very beautiful," she said with tremendous sincerity. "I don't think I've ever seen a woman as beautiful as you before."

I tried to frame a sensible answer to that, but she hurried down the stairs and out of sight before I could get the words out.

I went back to the bar walking on a cloud. I ordered another drink and went to the phone while the bartender was working on it. I dialed Pinocchio's.

"Yes?" said Andrew's sibilant voice.

"This is Penny," I said. "Do me a favor, Andrew?"

"Of course, dear. Name it."

"If Bernice should ask you anything about me, tell her I used to be an actress."

He burst into laughter. "But, darling—you are, you *are.*"

"Screw you," I said and hung up.

5.

MARCELLA HADN'T WAITED UP FOR ME, thank God. I was too overwrought to have faced any of her hurt-puppy questions about where I'd been. I know, of course, that I'd have to make some sort of excuse in the morning, but I would probably feel more up to it after a good night's sleep.

I undressed quickly and climbed into bed beside her. Marcella and I always slept in the nude, and I felt with distaste the bare length of one of her legs against my own as I slid in under the sheets.

She stirred and made a noise, and for a horrible moment I thought she was going to wake up. But she subsided again almost immediately. Marcella usually slept like a ton of bricks, and luckily this night was no exception.

I drew the sheets up over my naked body, feeling the brush of the crisp material against my breasts and loins, and snuggled my head into the pillow.

I thought about Bernice.

I simply couldn't get over the way things had gone between me and that girl. It hadn't even been necessary for me to form a plan of attack; Bernice had waltzed right into my arms as soon as I opened them. It was like slapping a tree with your palm and watching a whole goddamn peck of apples come tumbling down all around you. Better luck than *that* a girl just couldn't have.

Of course, it was always possible that I was overestimating my success. True, I had made friends with the girl and established a basis on which to extend that friendship in the direction I desired. But there was still no real reason for me to think Bernice would ever consent to warm a sheet with me. From what I could tell, she was probably still a virgin; she looked, acted and talked like one, and that big clod Mark seemed entirely too moral to have ever tried anything with her.

In a way, the fact of Bernice's virginity was an asset; an innocent is a lot easier to lead into sin than somebody who knows the score; but in another way, her lack of experience could handicap my scheme. It was possible that Bernice would blow sky-high the minute I laid my hands on her. As stupid as she might be, she would certainly recognize sex when she saw it, and it didn't take any significant amount of brains to realize that sex between two women was a trifle out of line.

Maybe I was counting my Bernices before they were hatched. I didn't think so, but I left the possibility open just in case. After all, if you're prepared for the worst, then nothing can ever take you by surprise.

With those two thoughts balancing in my mind, and with the image of Bernice standing between them—a mental picture of Bernice stripped naked, her breasts heaving with the anticipation of my caress, her mouth slack and sweet—I fell asleep.

I had this dream.

I don't know if *dream* is the right word, really. Dreams are supposed to be imaginings of the subconscious in which the mind is fooled into thinking that the senses are being stimulated. In a dream, you normally see and hear and feel more or less the way you do in reality, and the thing I experienced wasn't anything like that.

So it wasn't a dream.

But it wasn't a nightmare, either. Sometimes, a sleeping person will imagine all his senses are cut off, imagine he is deaf, dumb, blind, paralyzed, at the mercy of something he cannot see or even imagine. That's just about the worst sort of bad dream there is, but that wasn't what happened to me.

The only word I can think of to describe it is *impression*. It was a feeling of the mind, and it didn't involve sight or hearing or any of the senses.

I *felt* red, as if color had nothing to do with seeing, as if red were a huge looming object I could feel standing behind me, the way you do when you just know there's somebody looking over your shoulder even though they don't touch you or make any sound.

Red—not a color, then, but an impression; not anything I was experiencing, but a quality that was coming from inside me, a sense of redness that was part of my brain, my identity, part of the individual *me*.

Maybe none of this makes very much sense to you—it makes very little to me, when you come right down to it—but I can't describe it any other way. I was asleep, I was feeling red somehow or other, I wasn't dreaming, I wasn't conscious of myself or my life or the world—there was just this red inside me.

And it was growing. It was a pressure on my brain, a throbbing, a discomfort that was purely mental and had nothing to do with my physical self.

The red grew and grew, and it began to hurt, and I had to do something to release it, because it was dangerous. Like fire or lava, the red could burn me, scar me, twist me in agony unless I found a way to drain it off.

So I found a way. I did—I don't know—something or other, and the red flowed out of me, and the danger passed.

And then everything was all right again.

It hadn't been a dream. I didn't know at the time what it had been, but I didn't really care. As long as it was gone, as long as I was safe from it, who gives a damn?

Not me, certainly.

So I drifted away from the dream, or impression, or whatever it had been, and floated again back into the simple darkness of sleep.

When I woke up, it was almost noon.

The room was still as death, and I could tell from the feel of things that Marcella hadn't yet opened the store. There wasn't anything unusual about that, though; quite often, Marcella didn't begin the day's business until the middle of the afternoon.

I rolled my head on the pillow, expecting to find her beside me, but the bed was empty. I began to wonder if she'd gone out somewhere. Maybe I would be spared the discomfort of having to see her at all.

I started to push myself erect but stopped abruptly when a terrific pain ran up both my forearms. It was so unexpected and so intense that I guess I must have yelled aloud before letting my head fall back on the pillow.

Marcella appeared from out of nowhere beside the bed. She's like that with me; I swear, if I went to the opposite end of the Village and sneezed, she'd hear me and come running with a handkerchief.

"What is it, hon?" she asked, bending over me. "Are you all right?"

I had my eyes squeezed shut against the soreness of my arms, and I didn't answer her. Until that blasted pain passed, I didn't want to be bothered with anybody, much less Marcella.

"Can I get you something, hon?" Her voice was concerned, and there was a pleading note in it that was damned near as uncomfortable as the cramp in my arms.

"Leave me alone," I said, through clenched teeth. The pain was receding, but it was still very much there. I tried to move my fingers, but that only made it worse.

"Where does it hurt, honey?" Marcella persisted. "Tell me where it hurts, and I'll try to fix it for you."

She leaned forward even farther and put her hands on the bed. Her weight made the mattress give under me, causing my body to shift against one arm.

I howled. I couldn't help myself. I just hurt like hell and there wasn't a thing I could do about it.

"Is it your arm, honey? Is that what's hurting you?"

I pulled in a deep breath. "Yes, goddamn it," I shouted. "Stop leaning on the bed!"

She straightened quickly. The motion made me shift again, and again the rockets of pain went up my forearms.

"Wait," she said. "Don't move. I'll get something for you."

I felt her hand touch my cheek tenderly, then heard her footsteps moving away from the bed.

It was difficult to think with that terrible agony throbbing in my muscles, but I had the odd feeling that this
condition of my arms was a familiar thing, a thing which had
happened to me before. Sure . . . I was remembering now;
every once in a while, I would awaken like this, with my arms
all tied in knots, as if I had been through some terrific effort.
And usually, the sensation followed one of the red times,
followed that strange impression of redness and heat and
danger that sometimes invaded my sleep.

The pain in my arms and the redness. They were connected with something; they were important to me—not in
themselves, but because of their relationship to something
else . . .

I tried to pin the idea down, but it eluded me. I was too
sore to think clearly anyway. By the time Marcella had returned to my side, I had forgotten the train of thought
entirely.

She had a basin of hot water, some washcloths and towels and a tube of ointment. The pain had diminished enough
to allow me to open my eyes, and I watched her as she wet
one of the cloths and formed it gently around my arm.

It felt wonderful. The relief was immediate, and I knew
that it wouldn't be long before my arms were back to normal. But I didn't let Marcella know this; I didn't want to give
her the satisfaction of having helped me. The idea of being
in debt to anybody was repulsive; I've always felt that accept-
ing aid from another person diminished me, took the edge
off my natural superiority; and the thought of being in debt
to Marcella was doubly disgusting.

So, in spite of the relief flooding through my cramped
muscles as Marcella ministered tenderly to me, I kept up a

running string of complaints, told her several times she was just making it worse, bitched and whined over everything she did like a spoiled little kid.

As usual, it made no impression on Marcella whatsoever. She kept working on me tirelessly, and I imagine she would have continued for the whole afternoon if I hadn't finally recovered the use of my arms.

I pushed her away and sat up in bed. "That's enough," I said. "Give me a cigarette."

She set her equipment on the floor and crossed the room to the bureau, drying her hands on her skirt. She was wearing a dowdy housedress with flowers printed all over it. It did nothing at all for her figure, such as it was, and I imagined she was probably nude underneath it.

I was also naked, of course, and I considered pulling the sheets up over my shoulders before she returned to the bed. My body was bared from the top of my head all the way down to where my thighs began, and I wasn't sure it was a good idea to allow Marcella such a provocative eyeful. Then she turned and started back toward me; I looked directly into her face for the first time since I had awakened and noticed something that made me forget all about my nakedness.

"What's the matter with your face?" I asked.

She had started shaking two cigarettes out of her pack but stopped when she heard my question. One of her hands went up to touch a purplish bruise on her cheek. "Oh—this?" she said.

"Yes—that. And the other one." I nodded at a similar bruise on the other side of her face. "Your lip's split, too. How the hell did you do that?"

She smiled shallowly, nursing her lip. "I tripped," she said.

I snorted. "You look like you tripped out of a second-story window."

"No—it was the step you have to go up to get to the front of the store. You know the one." She shrugged. "I had just gotten up, and I was still sleepy—and I didn't see it, that's all."

I laughed. "Pretty stupid," I said.

She shrugged again. "Accidents happen."

"Only if you're stupid." I snapped my fingers. She lit a cigarette, handed it to me and sat down on the edge of the bed.

"How are your arms?" she asked.

"Better." I lifted them over my head and stretched my whole torso. I could see Marcella's eyes glutting themselves on my nudity, but for once I didn't really mind it. It was nice to know I still had the power to get the old butch excited. If I could do it to her, I could do it to others as well, like cuddly little Bernice, for example.

I reached behind me, hiked the pillow up between the headboard and my back and wriggled into a comfortable position. My breasts danced for Marcella. She was an appreciative audience.

"Strangest thing," I said.

She tore her eyes from my front with an effort. "What is, hon?"

"That business with my arms. I wonder why I get that?"

She drew on her cigarette. "It happens sometimes when you're asleep. I get cramps in my legs once in a while that are fierce enough to wake me up." Her expression changed slightly. "Especially if I've had a rough day—or a rough evening."

Here it comes, I thought. The quiet questions, the hurt looks, the sad eyes—the works. Marcella was an expert at turning that on, and once she hit her stride she could come on like a grieving mother whose son was on death row.

I tried to head her off. "Well, there wasn't anything about my evening rough enough to make me that sore. All I did was sit around Pinocchio's."

"Oh? Meet anyone?"

"Not a soul," I said. "I talked to Andrew for a while."

Marcella nodded thoughtfully. "I hear he has a new girl over there."

Damn her hide; apparently she had already learned about Bernice. Marcella was always up on the latest Village gossip, and more than once I had caught her looking at some new arrival on the scene with the obvious worry that she was in for some competition. She might suspect that I had my eye on Bernice, but unless that silly fag Andrew had spilled the beans, she couldn't have any proof.

"That's right," I said, very coolly. "A little blond girl, name of Bernice."

She puffed her cigarette. "What's she like?"

I smiled. "She's a clown," I said.

"Oh?"

"Just a young kid. Kind of pretty, but nothing on the ball. Stupid. You know what I mean."

"You talked to her, then?"

I cursed silently. "Only to order coffee. She waited on me. A real dumb little broad."

"I see." Marcella's face cleared a bit, and I knew she was beginning to believe me. Her suspicions were still alive, however; I had snowed her often enough in the past about my little friends.

"Anyway," I said, "I had a pretty dull evening. I might just as well have stayed home and watched you trip over things."

Marcella didn't answer. Her eyes were fixed again on my breasts.

And all of a sudden, I knew what was on her mind; and I also knew how her thoughts could be diverted from suspicions about my extracurricular activities into safer channels.

Marcella was in the mood.

As I let that idea sink in, I realized that I was also pretty much in the mood. I had gone through quite a bit of frustration with Bernice the previous evening, and the ache she had awakened in me hadn't found any sort of satisfaction. And while Marcella was certainly no Bernice from the standpoint of looks or personality, she was an accomplished old butch who knew all the tricks of giving a girl like me a good time.

Making it with Marcella would clear the air, and in more ways than one. It would satisfy her and it would also satisfy me; and that would free my mind for plotting my next move with Bernice. I knew from experience how hard it was to properly seduce anyone when my sex drive was in high gear.

"Marcella," I said.

"Huh?"

"What are you thinking about?"

She looked into my face. Her eyes skewed guiltily to one side. "Nothing," she said.

"Come on. You must have been thinking something or other. You were staring at me like I'd just stepped out of a flying saucer."

The tip of her tongue came out and wet her lips. It was a good sign. "I was thinking . . ."

"What, Marcella?"

"I was thinking how beautiful you are, Penny."

She didn't usually use my name in conversation. She liked to save it for times such as these. At that moment, I knew I had it made.

I sucked in a deep breath, making my rib cage flare and my tummy hollow. I passed my hands lightly over my tightened breasts. Marcella had never been able to resist a display like that, and this time was no exception.

"Do you really think I'm beautiful?" I asked softly.

"Oh. Penny." she said. "God—you know I do." Her excitement was growing, and it was making her face all loose and stupid. It was hard not to laugh at her when she looked like that.

"You didn't open the store yet, did you?" I asked her.

The change of subject seemed to puzzle her. "Why—no, I haven't."

"When are you?"

"I don't know. Later on."

"You don't have any definite time in mind?"

She shook her head. "No. Why do you ask?"

"I was just wondering." I paused and grinned at her. "If you're not in any hurry to open up—then we can have all the time we want, can't we?"

Her lips quivered. She wet them again. "Penny . . ."

"Why don't you take off that silly housedress, Marcella?"

She froze for a moment, torn between the desire to bare her body and the even stronger urge to grab me. Her features twitched and flickered like a badly made movie. Then, she rose from the bed and started undoing the front buttons of her housedress.

Her fingers were trembling terribly, and the sight of that pleased me. It was a great feeling to have someone in your power as thoroughly as I had Marcella. Her excitement was so intense that her whole body was palsied with it, and yet I hadn't done a thing but allow her to see me nude. The mere sight of what I had turned Marcella into mush, and you could hardly have a person more thoroughly in the palm of your hand than that.

As her housedress came open one button at a time, I felt an answering excitement blossoming inside myself. Marcella knew her stuff when it came to a bedroom romp and, when she was worked up as totally as she seemed to be now, she could play a symphony of pleasure on my flesh that would drive me straight out of my skull. A kick as big as that was worth looking forward to.

But aside from the anticipation of fun and games, and the satisfaction of my personal hungers, there was another element in our relationship; one which helped make all the delights of intimacy seem twice as big as life.

When I lay naked on a bed and allowed Marcella to crawl all over me, when I gave her hands and lips free rein over my flesh, when I returned the pleasure by caressing her in all the special ways she'd taught me—when I did all that, I *owned* Marcella. I was the Master—or Mistress, if you prefer—and she was my goddamn slave, a creature set down on earth for the simple purpose of entertaining and taking care of *me*.

She was mine, to do with as I pleased. If I chose to give her what she yearned for, that decision was my own, and the delights she enjoyed came exclusively from me. I could just as easily withhold myself from her, make her ache with unfulfilled desire, drive her to her knees with nothing more than the power of my naked body.

I could give her pleasure, or I would give her pain. I controlled her utterly. Where Marcella was concerned, I was God.

Her housedress slithered to the floor. As I had suspected, she was naked beneath it.

She had an odd build—not pretty, but not really ugly, either. She looked a bit like a squarely built adolescent boy on whom somebody had hung several areas of un-masculine curves. Her breasts were very large, bigger by far than my own, but in spite of their weight and her age they stood forth with remarkable firmness. They were round and white, tipped with enormous brownish circles.

Her waist was tight, her belly smooth, the curves of her hips degraded by the faint protrusions of her bony pelvis, her thighs a bit too heavy for real beauty.

All in all, she didn't really look like a woman—she looked exactly like what she was.

A lesbian.

And that suited me fine.

I slid down flat onto the bed and kicked the sheets away. I held out my arms toward her.

"Come and get it, Marcella."

She came forward like a woman in a dream and knelt on the bed beside my hips. I put my hand on one of her thighs, then slid it up and around until I was holding one of her buttocks.

"Oh, Penny," she said. "I want you so much. I'd do anything for you, honey. Anything."

I arched my back. My breasts rose toward her invitingly. "That's big talk," I said.

"I mean it, Penny."

I tightened my grip on her bottom. "Show me," I said.

She sprawled forward.

I felt her huge breasts settle against my belly. Her hands cupped me, her breath blew hot into my cleavage. She was muttering something I couldn't hear, but I could feel her words as little individual moistures against my flesh and knew exactly what she was saying.

Her face shifted. Her hands curled around the perimeter of my left breast. When she spoke, her breath caressed the stiffening coin of the tip.

"Penny," she said.

Then her mouth had me, and the world went away.

I wrapped my arms around her neck, drawing her lips tightly against my flesh. A faint echo of pain chased through the muscles of my forearms.

But I couldn't stop to worry about that. Marcella was doing her best for me, and her best was simply terrific. In the midst of such pleasure the idea of pain had no place at all.

So I gave myself over to her completely. And all the while she kissed and caressed my naked body, I pretended she was Bernice.

6.

THAT EVENING, I went to Pinocchio's again.

The session with Marcella had done wonders for my disposition, and it had also helped me form a plan of seduction which, I was sure, would eventually net me Bernice. It would take a bit of work and quite a bit of waiting, but I knew I was on the right track. And I had left Marcella glowing and happy back at the shop, with all her hungers satisfied, all her suspicions erased by pleasure, so even that part of my life was ordered and arranged as it should be.

I felt just great.

Pinocchio's wasn't nearly as crowded as it had been the night before. I looked for Bernice as I walked in, but I didn't see her anywhere. I saw Andrew, though, and he saw me. The familiar dirty smile lit up his whole face.

"Darling," he said, as I came down to his counter. "Such a pleasure to see you again. It isn't often these poor premises are graced by the presence of such a well-known and glamorous actress as yourself."

"Where's Bernice?" I asked.

"Working in the ladies' washroom, dear. Replacing the paper towels."

"I thought you took care of the ladies' room yourself."

"Don't be nasty, darling. After all, I'm on your side."

I leaned my elbows on the counter. "Has she been asking about me?"

"My dear," Andrew said, "she's talked of nothing else ever since she came on duty this afternoon. I've answered so many questions in the past few hours, I feel as if I'm under investigation."

"What have you told her—exactly?"

He filled me in. He'd done a pretty good job, considering the fact that he hadn't known the details of the conversation I'd had with Bernice. He'd dragged from her the skeleton of my snow-job, then fleshed it out with details of his own. Thanks to him, Bernice now believed that I had done musical comedy, contemporary drama, Shakespeare and poetry readings, which was a hell of a career to have spanned only two seasons of summer stock.

"Andrew, don't you think you laid it on a little thick?"

He looked hurt. "Now, dear, you must have a higher opinion of me than that. I told that girl only what she wanted to hear. I let her lead the way. Believe me, she's so thoroughly enraptured with you that she's willing to accept virtually any piece of information, no matter how preposterous."

I laughed. "You missed your calling, Andrew."

"Did I?"

"Sure. With a line like that, you should have been a heterosexual."

"My dear," he simpered, "so should you." He winked at me and turned back to his work.

It was a temptation to go back to the ladies' john and corner Bernice, but I controlled it. Sitting on my urges was out of character for me, but I knew it would be necessary for the successful completion of my campaign. I figured the more practice I got, the better I would be at it.

So I went to the phone booth at the front of the place and made a few calls.

People live a free and easy life in the Village. Many of the local inhabitants are writers, poets, artists or shop-owners of some sort and are therefore their own bosses. As a consequence of the fact that they have no employer cracking the whip over them, Village people throw more parties than you'd believe. There's hardly a night in the week when you can't find at least one full-scale bash going on, and usually there are several.

I started by phoning some of the girls I'd had fun with in the past. I was on friendly terms with most of my former lovers, and I tried to keep things that way. I didn't relish the idea of getting any of them mad enough at me to go tattle to Marcella.

I called Lydia—a swarthy, hard-bodied dancer with whom I'd jazzed about a year earlier. She was a little too tough and dirty-mouthed for my tastes, although there was no denying her technique in the sack.

She wasn't home.

Next, I called Tracy. She was a fashion model, one of those impossibly willowy creatures who always seem so flat-chested and sexless in the magazines. Relieved of those high-fashion clothes, however, Tracy was anything but flat-chested—she had a pair of breasts like hard, round little apples—and she was far from sexless. Tracy and I had balled for three months steady a while back, before she had taken up with a neurotic little female folk-singer from San Francisco.

Tracy wasn't home either.

I called Brandy—a big girl who rubbed matron-fat all day at a ladies' reducing salon; I called Solveig—who got her money by posing nude for male photographers and got her kicks by posing nude for girls like me; I called Joyce—who worked on the staff of a man's magazine and was a better judge of suggestive stories and pictures than any of her male co-workers.

None of them were home.

I glanced through the glass doors of the booth and saw that Bernice had come out of the john and returned to work. I forced myself not to look at her and dialed another number. If I couldn't connect before Bernice noticed my presence, then the whole evening would be shot.

I called Fred as a last resort. He was, as his name implied, a man; in fact, one of the few males I'd ever had an affair with. Fred was a big, good-looking guy, and there was no hint in either his face or his manner of the boiling mess of neuroses he was inside. He made his living playing bass with small jazz combos around town. And, if you're really interested, he was lousy in bed.

The phone rang five times before it was answered. The moment the receiver was off the hook, I knew I had hit the jackpot. The unmistakable bellow of a party in full swing was so loud in the receiver that I could barely hear Fred's voice.

"Who?" he yelled.

"Penny Stewart," I said. "You throwing a bash?"

"No," he said, "just spending a quiet evening at home. That noise you hear is bomb tests."

"Am I invited?"

"Everybody's invited," he shouted. "I think everybody in the world is already here except you."

"Good. I'll be over in a while. Oh—and one more thing."

"Yeah?"

"Can I bring a friend?"

He laughed. "Do you have one?"

"Funny," I said. I hung up.

I felt like a million bucks when I came out of that phone booth and headed for a table.

Bernice's face lighted when she saw me. I sat down and gestured her over; she came like a moth to a candle. Behind her, I could see Andrew grinning at us from ear to ear.

It was only when Bernice had sat down opposite me that I noticed how different she looked. She'd untied her ponytail and her hair now fell straight and clear to her shoulders, framing her innocent face in cascades of pure gold. She was wearing lipstick, but she'd had enough sense to pick out a delicate coral shade that accented the sensuous line of her mouth.

Most fascinating of all, however, was her choice of clothing. Gone was the bulky sweater and heavy skirt; in their place, she wore a frilly white blouse, which hugged the mounds of her breasts deliciously, and a simple skirt cut tightly enough to show me that my speculations about her trim hips and thighs had been pretty accurate.

She looked simply terrific, and I felt good when I realized that she had probably horsed herself up for my benefit.

"Hi, Penny," she said. Her voice was gusty with happiness.

"Hello, Bernice." I fastened my best smile in place and reached across the table to touch her hand. "How have you been?"

"Wonderful," she said. "I haven't been able to get my mind off what we talked about last night. I just can't wait to start. I . . ." She dipped her head. "I asked Andrew about you—I hope you don't mind."

"Of course not, Bernice. Why should I?"

She grinned at me. "You certainly were modest last night."

"I was?"

"Sure. You never said anything about playing Shakespeare or those poetry readings. I'll bet you read poetry wonderfully."

"Thanks," I said. Andrew was right; this kid would swallow anything. And that quality was the biggest asset a victim could have.

"Penny?" she said, interrupting my happy thoughts. "I don't want to rush you, or anything, but—"

"Say what's on your mind, Bernice."

"Well, as I explained to you last night, there's a time limit on my making good. I'm really very anxious to get started."

I had to think for a second before I remembered that I'd promised her acting lessons. "Oh, of course," I said. "I haven't forgotten about that. But there are a few things I have to line up first before we can get started."

Her disappointment showed clearly on her face. "I see. I'd hoped . . ."

"Don't get me wrong, Bernice," I said quickly. "I'm not trying to put you off. Remember, the acting lessons were only part of our deal."

"I don't understand."

"I promised to introduce you to some people."

Her features cleared. "Yes—that's important, too, isn't it?"

"Damn right," I said. "In a way, *who* you know is more important than *what* you know."

"When can I meet some of these people?"

I smiled casually. "How about tonight?"

"*Tonight!* You really mean it?"

"Certainly. There's a party going on not far from here. I've got an invitation for the both of us."

"How wonderful," she said.

"Now, don't get too excited," I said. "Not everybody there will be connected with show business. I can't guarantee anything."

"Oh, that's all right," she said happily. "I'm not expecting miracles. But just making some friends in the Village ought to help me along, don't you think?"

"The right kind of friends are the best assets a girl can have," I said, my voice just syrupy enough to sound sincere.

She lapped it up. "Then I guess I'm very lucky to have met you," she said.

"We'll see about that," I replied. "Can you come to the party with me?"

"Sure, I can. I wouldn't miss it for the world."

"What time do you get off work tonight?"

"I'm supposed to keep at it until eleven o'clock—but things are slow this evening. Maybe Andrew would let me off early."

I patted her hand again. "I'll go talk to him, put in a good word for you."

"Thanks," she said. "You're awfully good to me, Penny."

"Think nothing of it. Now—what about Mark?"

A small shadow passed across her face. "What about him?"

"Is he coming down to meet you again tonight?"

"I don't know. I haven't talked to him since last night. But he probably is going to be waiting for me when I quit."

I said my next words very slowly and carefully, hoping I was on the right track. "If you leave early, Bernice, you might miss him."

She stared into space for a moment, and her pretty features underwent several subtle changes. I could see the various thoughts chasing through her head as clearly as if her skull had been made of glass. I waited.

She turned her eyes back to me finally, and all at once her face was illuminated by a lovely smile.

"Who cares about him?" she said.

I pushed my chair back from the table and stood up quickly. "I'll go talk to Andrew," I said.

He was a fag, he had a dirty mind and he could be pretty much of a pain in the neck at times, but Andrew was a great man to have on your side when you were planning something nasty. He let Bernice off two hours early without a whimper—and even promised to pay her for the full evening. All the while he was informing her of his munificence, his eyes kept looking at me, and the messages which passed silently between us couldn't have been printed anywhere but on a public lavatory wall.

We left Andrew lisping his hopes that we would have a good time and headed across the Village toward Fred's apartment.

Bernice gabbed happily all the way over, but I wasn't listening to her. I was a bit worried about one phase of my plan. As far as I knew, there wouldn't be a single soul at the party who could qualify as a member of show business, except for Fred who was a musician. If Bernice circulated in that mob, talked to enough people, asked a few of the wrong questions, she might tumble to the fact that I was pulling her leg. And that would put both me and my plans so far up the creek that we could never get down again. Bringing Bernice to that party might be the biggest mistake I ever made.

I felt reassured, though, when I recalled the racket I'd heard over the phone. A party making that much noise had reached the stage where it would swallow people whole, plunging them into the midst of pleasure and excitement, giving them no chance to even introduce themselves, much less ask questions. A lot would depend, of course, on just who was there, but I was pretty sure things would work out my way.

As it turned out, I was absolutely right.

The party was going at such a pitch when Bernice and I arrived that I could see immediately she would have no opportunity to get a sensible word out of anyone. As I dragged her into Fred's apartment and began the introductions, I realized another factor in my favor; Bernice was too awed and confused by the scene to even attempt a conversation on her own.

Everything was working for me, and it was a marvelous sensation.

All the girls who'd been out when I called were there at Fred's party. I introduced Bernice to Brandy, the reducing-salon masseuse, and watched the big girl's gaze appraise my little prize with frank admiration. Brandy was wild enough to try something if the chance arose, and I steered Bernice away from her quickly.

I showed off Bernice to Joyce, the girl who worked on the man's magazine. Joyce was impressed. She asked Bernice if she had ever considered posing in the nude for a magazine spread, and I had a little trouble smoothing that one over. But Bernice was too stunned to understand much of anything that went on, and I made it away from Joyce without any further incident.

Lydia, the dancer, was bombed out of her mind when I brought Bernice over to her. I could tell by the glazed condition of her eyes, and I thought she was high on alcohol until I spotted the shaggy homemade cigarette in her hand. My nostrils picked up the unmistakable smell of pot—marijuana to those of you who don't dig the idiom—and I knew that Lydia was on her way into orbit. I hadn't realized it was going to be that sort of party. I hoped Bernice wouldn't tip to what was going on and get turned off by it.

Tracy, the fashion model, and Solveig, the photographer's model, were off by themselves in a corner of the room. Luckily, I spotted them before Bernice did and managed to get her out of range before she saw the torrid embrace they were sharing. From the looks of the hanky-panky in that corner, Tracy and Solveig would be stripped down and posing for each other before the evening was over.

I located Fred finally. He was also high on weed, but not as obviously so as Lydia. He said a casual hello to me and Bernice, told a hilarious dirty joke about a jazz musician and an elephant, then veered off into another corner of the party, leaving Bernice shocked and tickled.

Before she had any opportunity to recover from that, I poured a good stiff drink and shoved it into her hand. She took a healthy swallow, and things really started to get rolling.

I was prepared to make up all sorts of lies about the people at that party, but Bernice didn't ask any questions. She acted quite enchanted with the noise and color of the group. She'd led such a sheltered life that I guess those hopped-up Village loonies looked as glamorous to her as a pack of movie stars; whatever it was, I could see she was dreaming the dreams I had planned for her, and with no help from me at all.

The party passed in a haze. It was quite a while before Bernice could summon enough nerve to talk to anyone, and even then she did nothing but make polite conversation. Some of the people we gabbed with had sex on the brain—a customary brain affliction in the Village—but fortunately most of the allusions were too far out to make any impression on Bernice. She smiled and nodded at everything that was said, whether she understood it or not, and worked doggedly down to the bottom of her drink. I made sure she got a prompt refill.

Things were coming along beautifully.

And then, something happened that was more beautiful than all the rest put together.

Brandy and Joyce got into an argument over breasts.

It was a stupid argument, but they were both drunk enough to go at it as if it really meant something. Brandy's work as a masseuse had given her a strong-muscled frame but hadn't blurred any of her obvious femininity. Her breasts were as pretty a pair of globes as had ever filled a blouse, and she wore them proudly the way some women wear jewels. Joyce was also a good-looking woman, but in a different way. Her development was just as shapely but softer, more yielding, somehow more tender.

So that's what the argument was about. Brandy maintained that a woman's body hadn't reached its fullest potential until all the muscles had been properly developed. Joyce, on the other hand, maintained that muscle had nothing to do with it, that she herself didn't have a well-developed muscle in her entire body but would be willing to match her figure against anyone's. Brandy flaunted her firm frontage in support of her contention, Joyce thrust what she had hard against her blouse in rebuttal, and the argument reached a stalemate.

I looked around and discovered I wasn't the only one watching Brandy and Joyce. Almost everyone in the room had turned to watch them, and conversation was dying as the nature of their argument sank in. A number of people were laughing, and some were making ribald comments in attempt to buy into the argument.

All at once, some girl I'd never seen before made this delightful suggestion: If Brandy and Joyce were so concerned over their comparative bust development, why didn't they take their breasts out in the open and compare them? That way, without a blouse to conceal or a bra to uplift, their breasts would have to stand or fall entirely on their own merits.

The girl's suggestion was greeted with shouts of approval from everyone, including myself. Beside me, I felt Bernice stiffen.

"Penny—they're not *really* going to take off their clothes, are they?"

"Sure, they are," I said lightly. "How else can they settle the argument?"

"But—that's wrong." She was frowning. "Girls shouldn't show themselves that way."

I turned toward her and took her hands. "All right, Bernice, I guess it's time for your first lesson. You want to be an actress, don't you?"

"Well—yes."

"And an actress is somebody who plays a role, who uses her face and her body to create an illusion on a stage. Right?"

"Yes," she said.

"Now, suppose you were afraid to let people see your face. Suppose you couldn't walk on a stage unless you were wearing a mask. What kind of actress would you be?"

"Not a very good one, I suppose."

"That's right," I said. "And the same thing goes for your body."

"But—"

"No buts. A good actress can play Queen Victoria in full dress or Lady Godiva in the nude. It doesn't make any difference to her. When you're an actress, your face and body are just props for you to work with, the tools of your profession. It has nothing to do with indecency or embarrassment.

If you let emotions like that get between you and your audience, you'll never establish any sort of contract with them."

"But Penny, this isn't a stage. This is just a party."

"True," I said. "And nobody's asking you to do anything, are they? Those two girls over there are busy with their own business. Nudity doesn't make them uncomfortable. They have the attitude of the true actress, and if they feel like taking off their blouses to settle the argument, that's their concern."

Bernice's face was growing a bit red. "I don't know whether I should watch."

"You don't have to," I said. "But it might be better if you did. The sooner you get used to the idea there's nothing terrifying about the human body, clothed or naked, the sooner you're going to get the knack of using that body the way an actress should."

She nodded. Her eyes looked rather filmy, and I could tell that the liquor was working in her. "I guess you're right. If you say it's okay."

"It is, believe me. Watch and see."

I held onto her hand and turned back toward Joyce and Brandy.

Joyce had already removed her blouse and was busy unhooking her bra. It would be a pleasure to see her breasts again; I remembered them quite well from the blasts we'd shared a couple of years before. As her brassiere came off, I was gratified to see that she was in as good shape as ever. The twin beauties rode on her elegant torso as delicately as if they had no weight to them at all. I recalled how malleable they had been in my hands, and the memory sent a chill through my intestines. Joyce's flesh wasn't at all muscular, but it was as beautifully curved as any woman's flesh could be.

Brandy was wearing a one-piece dress. When she unzipped the back and dropped it to her waist, it slipped out of her fingers and fell all the way to the floor. She didn't bother to retrieve it. When she removed her brassiere, her only remaining garments were her panties and a sheer half-slip. Brandy's breasts looked hard as rock. They stood from her body without a trace of sag or softness, and the ridged discs of her small nipples stood far enough out of her flesh to cast tiny shadows beneath them. I had felt those breasts, too, several months back, and I had no trouble remembering how bouncy and resilient they had been.

Joyce's set was pretty in a particular way, Brandy's was just as pretty but in a different way. The argument was pointless—that is, as an argument.

But as a way of loosening up Bernice, the scene could hardly have been better if I'd staged it myself.

The two girls were still yelling at each other. Brandy grabbed her nude bust in her hands and pivoted around, showing everybody how solid she was. This display was met with a round of applause.

Then Joyce did the same thing, weighing her paired softnesses in both palms, showing the crowd that a woman could be shapely without being hard. They applauded for her just as vigorously.

I stole a glance at Bernice and found her staring at those two half-naked girls with intense fascination. The look of excitement on her face made me tremble.

When I glanced back, another girl had joined the discussion. The one who had made the original suggestion to strip was standing beside Brandy and Joyce and was in the process of stripping herself. She was yelling that size rather than shape was the determining factor where breasts were concerned and she told both girls quite brazenly that she thought they were overblown. She called them cows, but before that remark could start a fight, she had stripped off her bra and was showing the room what she meant.

Her breasts were simply luscious. They were no larger than a half-grapefruit and just as symmetrical. When she moved, they didn't sway or jiggle but flexed with her motion like round, soft muscles.

That did it. The party was really getting in the mood now. Just about every girl in the place was on her feet and peeling, anxious to join the competition. Breasts were spilling free of their confinements all over the room, and the sight of it was enough to dry all the spit from my mouth. I felt the colossal urge to tear off my own blouse and join the fun—it certainly looked as if the party was on its way to becoming a first-rate orgy—but I checked the impulse when I remembered Bernice.

I looked at her. When I saw what she was doing, my eyes nearly fell out of my head.

She was staring at the naked girl-flesh all around her with an expression of hypnotized concentration. Her fingers had unbuttoned her blouse all the way down to the waist. She shrugged each shoulder in turn, and the blouse rode down her arms.

Before I could say a word to stop her, she had unhooked her brassiere, shaken her breasts free and was rising to join in.

Everything stopped. All around the room, heads turned to look at her. Even girls who were in the middle of disrobing paused to take her in.

That's how beautiful she was. I couldn't recall ever having seen such a beautiful set of breasts—so round and high, and at the same time so soft-looking and tender. Her body had a youthful, almost childish look to it, but her curves were pure woman.

She moved forward into the center of the room dreamily. The smiling mob cleared a space for her. She stopped and stood for a long moment without moving, and I got the impression that she had totally forgotten where she was.

Then, slowly, she started to dance.

Let me tell you, it was something to behold. I guess my words about the free and easy use of the body as an instrument of the dramatic art had really taken root in her mind, because she was using that body with more effect than any woman I had ever seen. My heart came lurching up into my throat as she shimmied and swayed, moving her breasts and arms and shoulders in time to some private jungle rhythm inside her. It was glorious to watch, but it was painfully frustrating, too. Seeing her like that made me want to leap from my chair, grab her and go straight out of my mind. But I had enough sense left to know that wouldn't be a good idea in the midst of such a mob.

But I wasn't the only one being affected by her dance. Without any warning, a young man had suddenly jumped from his chair and was reaching out for her.

I was on my feet in an instant. Time seemed to slow down, and my feet dragged maddeningly as I tried to get between them before his curling fingers could close around those sweet breasts. The fingers touched her, just grazing the tips, and Bernice's eyes went wide.

My hand flailed out and slapped the young guy across the face. The flesh of his cheeks jiggled loosely, and I noticed that he was too high on pot to even know he'd been hit. He weaved backward, looking slightly bewildered by it all.

I got behind Bernice and grabbed both her breasts in my hands, to conceal them from the eyes of that ravenous crowd, of course.

"All right," I shouted. "That's enough. You lousy stud, leave this girl alone."

Bernice was breathing heavily. Her flesh swelled into my palms.

"Penny," she said.

"We better get out of here, Bernice," I said into her ear. "Some of these young men can't be trusted."

I walked her back to where her clothing was, released her breasts reluctantly and helped her get dressed. My big scene hadn't made much impression on the group. Now that the pretty little blonde was covered up, they seemed anxious to get back to their original business—the process of working up to a mass orgy.

The girls were taking off their skirts and a few of the boys were also busily undressing by the time I managed to get Bernice out of there. I heard a few nasty remarks flung after me about how unfair I was to keep such a tasty plum to myself, but I ignored them, and Bernice was too dazed to catch their meaning.

I got her down onto the street and urged her toward the nearest bar. I knew I would have to talk fast in order to keep this incident from making her hysterical and ruining everything. Above all, I had to stay calm, had to appear completely certain of myself.

And that was going to be damned hard with the sensation of her naked breasts still tingling in my hands.

7.

"I CAN'T UNDERSTAND IT," Bernice was saying. "Why on earth did I ever do such a thing?"

We were sitting together in a bar not far from Pinocchio's. It was late, and we had the rear booths all to ourselves. Bernice's speech was still a bit slushy, but she had recovered her wits sufficiently to realize what she had done at the party.

At the moment, she was more bewildered than frightened, and I was working like hell to make sure she stayed that way.

"Bernice, there wasn't a thing wrong with what you did. If it hadn't been for that grabby young guy, everything would have been fine."

"But—but I took off my bra." Her face twitched. "I let them all see my breasts—all naked. I danced for them. I don't know *why* I did that."

"Would you like me to tell you?"

"Yes, Penny, please. I'm all mixed up inside."

"There's nothing so hard to understand about it," I said. "You just wanted to entertain them."

"Entertain?"

"Of course. It was a perfectly natural instinct, under the circumstances—natural, that is, for a girl who really wants to be an actress and who has what it takes."

She sighed, and the tightness of her features eased a trifle. You'll have to explain that to me, Penny. I'm not following you."

"All right," I said. "Let's take it one step at a time. You went to a party tonight—a party of complete strangers. You didn't know a soul there except me. Right?"

"Go on."

"Everything was going along calmly and normally until Brandy and Joyce started arguing about their breasts."

"Were those the two girls? I didn't catch their names."

I nodded. "Now, I'll grant you their argument was pretty silly, but so what? In their way, they were just having some fun with each other. They felt like showing off, calling a little attention to themselves. There's nothing very oddball about that."

"I guess not."

"Both Joyce and Brandy, by the way, have worked in show business," I lied. "Maybe I didn't tell you that."

"No, you didn't."

"Well, it's a fact. They're both used to thinking of their bodies as part of their trade, not as anything secret or personal, and certainly not as anything to be hidden. As it happened, they both felt that taking off their blouses was the only way to settle their argument—so that's what they did."

"I see," Bernice said, as if she didn't see at all.

"Bernice—the only reason you're having trouble following this is because you've got what they did all mixed up in your mind with sex."

"Sex?"

"Certainly. After all, when a person removes their clothes in the presence of another person, more often than not sex is the reason behind it. But not always, Bernice. In this particular case, I don't imagine either Joyce or Brandy gave any thought at all to sex."

That, incidentally, was a bald-faced lie. Knowing the two girls as well as I did, I was quite certain they'd started that argument with the express purpose of sending the party off the deep end. I kept a straight face while Bernice pondered what I'd said.

"Maybe not," she said. "But some of the others were."

"Exactly. And that's what fouled things up. If it hadn't been for a few dirty minds in the audience, there wouldn't have been any trouble."

She nodded. I could tell that my use of the word *audience* had made an impression. She was thinking of the party in terms of a stage. It was a big step in the right direction.

"So," I hurried on, "Brandy and Joyce took off their blouses. They did it because they felt like it and not to excite anyone. Basically, I guess they did it to entertain the others, to cheer them up and make them laugh."

"Yes," Bernice said. "I can understand how that might be."

"Okay. Now, the next thing that happened was when that other girl got up. I don't have any idea who she was, but I know the type. The limelight was on Joyce and Brandy, and she was jealous. She decided to claim some attention for herself by moving in on their act."

Bernice nodded again.

"She took off her blouse," I said, "and right away that meant three girls in the room had their breasts exposed. And, as the saying goes, three is a crowd."

"What?" She looked perplexed.

"By that, I mean that when three people do a thing, the people around them will usually start considering seriously whether or not to join them. It's the herd instinct. People want to be accepted, and the best way to guarantee that is to act as much like everybody else as you possibly can."

"I know all about that," said Bernice. "The town I come from, the people I knew there—they were all that way. Conformists. If enough people did a thing, they'd do it, too, whether they wanted to or not."

"Now you've got the idea, Bernice. All those other girls joined in and started peeling because they wanted to move with the mob. Conformity isn't really a good thing, but it's not all that bad, either."

"Conformists," said Bernice again. "Like me."

"You?"

"Yes, *me,*" she said heatedly. "Didn't I do the same thing everyone else did? Didn't I take off my blouse and my bra and get up and try to attract attention to myself? Am I any better than they are?"

She acted as if she were working up to a real fit, and I moved in quickly to calm her down.

"No," I said. "You did what you did for an entirely different reason. The way you acted set you apart from the herd, and, incidentally, convinced me that you have some pretty unique gifts."

For the first time since we had left the party, I saw her face smooth out. A tentative smile tugged at the corners of her mouth. "You're just saying that."

"I mean it, Bernice. I don't think you yourself know why you peeled and joined the fun. But I do."

"Tell me why, Penny." She laced her fingers and leaned forward across the table.

"All right. It's like this. With all those girls naked to the waist and showing themselves off, that room became something more than a room—it became a stage. They were all performing, to one degree or another, even though they wouldn't have admitted it, not even to themselves. They wanted attention, they wanted people to see them and admire them. They saw an easy way to make that happen, so they took it."

"But how was I any different, Penny? I took the same opportunity they did."

"The opportunity may have been the same, but what you *did* with it was way out of their league. All they'd done was show off their breasts." I paused a moment for effect. "But you danced."

"I danced," she said quietly.

"The instinct of a real actress," I said. "You got out there and cut them all dead. You took that situation and made it your own."

"Did I really do that, Penny?"

"You bet your life you did. The minute you started doing your dance, that whole room shut up. I don't think there was a soul in there who wasn't looking right at you. It was great."

"I remember," she said stupidly. "I could feel their eyes on me, and I wanted to do something for them, to give them something to look at. Is that what you mean?"

"That's exactly what I mean. You weren't just going to stand around and show off your flesh. You wanted to perform. That's what made the difference."

She gnawed her lip. "Penny?"

"What?"

"Did I look good?"

"You'd better believe it, Bernice."

"I mean, did I do it well? Was I just jumping around and making a fool of myself, or was I really doing something worth watching?"

"Bernice, you looked absolutely beautiful. Your body was beautiful, and what you did with it was even more beautiful. I could have sat there and watched you forever."

"Thanks," she said, bobbing her head.

"It's the truth."

All of a sudden, she giggled. "You know—I was a little bit tipsy, Penny."

"Oh?"

"I don't think I would have had nerve enough to do such a thing without a few drinks in me beforehand."

"Well, it was the first time you ever tried it, Bernice. Nerve comes with experience in situations like that."

She smiled. "It felt funny to be in the nude where everybody could see me. It was kind of nice."

The tone of her voice made me shiver. It was time to play my last card.

"Bernice," I said. "I would have watched you all night and loved every minute of it, if that young punk hadn't tried that smart business."

Her smile fell. "That was terrible," she said. "I didn't even know he was there until I felt him touch my—touch me." She stared at me intently. "It's a good thing you were there to protect me, Penny. That's the second time you've helped me out of a spot. I owe you quite a bit."

"Bernice, let me ask you something."

"Of course."

"The good feeling you say you had—the nice feeling of being in the nude where people could look at you—when did that go away?"

"When he touched me," she said.

"I thought so. And do you know why his touch killed all the fun for you?"

She frowned. "No."

"Because he changed what you were doing from entertainment to sex."

She nodded slowly. "Yes . . . that's right. I remember thinking that. I felt his hands on me, and all of a sudden I realized that I was doing something sexy. And I got scared."

"Sure, you did," I said, patting her arm. "And you had every right to be. That's why I got you away from there as quickly as I could. Some of these young guys can be real animals, and I didn't want you to get hurt."

"It wasn't so bad being naked," she said thoughtfully. "But having somebody touch me that way . . ." She shuddered.

"Bernice?"

"Yes?"

"*I* touched you. Remember?"

A curious expression grew on her face. "Yes . . . you did, didn't you?"

"I put my hands over your breasts to keep those swine from looking at them. It was the only way I could think of to conceal you."

"Thanks again," she said.

"How did it feel when I touched you, Bernice? The same as when that boy did it, or what?"

"Oh, no—completely different. When you put your hands on me, I felt—I felt *safe*. I felt as if nothing could hurt me as long as you were holding me that way." Her gaze faltered. "You were very gentle, Penny."

I took a deep breath. "So, you see, it wasn't the touch at all, any more than it was the nudity. Being naked isn't bad in itself. Letting somebody touch your naked flesh isn't bad, either. But it all depends on the reason behind the nakedness and the touching."

"Yes," she said. "I can see that."

"Feeling that boy's hands on you made you afraid, because you knew what he had in mind. But feeling my hands on you felt comforting, because you knew I wasn't going to hurt you. Can you see that difference?"

"Yes," she said.

"It's the difference between a man and a woman, Bernice. Men are rough. Women are gentle. That's all there is to it."

"I never looked at it that way before," she said.

"Think about it," I told her. "Keep it in mind the next time you see Mark."

I took her to the subway and fired her uptown, satisfied with my evening's work. On the way back to Marcella's I congratulated myself on a job well done. Of course, fate had been working overtime to co-operate with me, but the bulk of my success could be attributed to the way I'd used each advantage.

Without half trying, I'd brought Bernice a giant-step closer to the crossroads. She knew now what it was like to bare her body in the presence of others. She knew the exhilarating feeling of knowing eyes were looking at her, approving of her, stirred by what they saw.

She knew how shocking and terrible the touch of a man could be in such a situation.

She also knew how sweet and tender the touch of a woman could be under the same circumstances.

I'd actually held Bernice's naked breasts right in my own two hands, but that was the smallest of the evening's victories. Three new ideas were now planted in her stupid blond head, and they had already started to take root:

Nudity can be fun.

The touch of a man can be repulsive.

The caress of a woman can be a delight.

I whistled all the way home, which was something I hadn't done in years.

8.

THE ATMOSPHERE OF CALM AND TRUST at Marcella's didn't last.

My enthusiastic love-making had soothed the old broad briefly, but it didn't take long for the memory of that to fade from her mind, leaving room for the regrowth of all her suspicions.

The morning after the party, when I came up front into the shop, I sensed the change in Marcella immediately. Her face was set in sour lines, and she hardly answered me when I said good morning. She opened the place for the day, and we went to work. I kept my eye on her, watching to see if her mood was improving or worsening, trying to catch some clue as to the nature of her thoughts. But I didn't have any luck. Her features remained stony, and all I could tell for certain was that I was going to be in for some trouble with Marcella.

Not that the idea bothered me particularly; I had always been able to handle anything Marcella dished out. She and I had had fights before, usually over my playing around, and I had always managed to smooth things down before any real trouble developed.

But Marcella could be pretty nasty when she got the idea I was cheating on her. I swear, she acted sometimes as if she were my goddamned husband. Sure, she supported me, took care of me, shared her bed and her body with me, but that didn't give her any permanent claim to my affections. She was damned lucky I consented to live with her at all; if I ever skipped out on her, she'd have a hell of a time finding anybody to replace me.

No matter how noisy our fights got, though, I was careful never to remind her of that fact. As I said before, Marcella was the sort of romantic idiot who could imagine she was in love with her lesbian girlfriend; and, considering all I'd gotten from her and all I stood to get if I didn't rock the boat, I would be an even worse idiot to spoil her illusions.

At the moment, there was nothing to do but ride with the situation, work around the shop like a good girl and wait to see if Marcella's mood would pass. It irked me having to keep my trap shut in the face of her cruddy anger, and several times I was on the verge of telling her off and saying the hell with the whole setup. But somehow, I got through the day without causing the tension between us to flare into anything worse. By evening, I began to think maybe the storm would pass without ever having broken.

Perhaps it would have, too, if not for that goddamned phone call.

I was arranging some dresses on a rack when I heard the ringing from the back room. Marcella went to answer it. She was closer to the rear, for one thing, and since most of my little friends knew better than to call me at the shop, the phone rarely rang for me.

Marcella disappeared into the back. I returned my attention to my work. I hadn't gotten very far when I heard her call my name.

"Penny."

"Yes?"

"It's for you."

My hands froze around a hanger. A variety of thoughts scampered through my mind, all of them grim, and I cursed the luck that had brought me a call at such an inopportune moment. The tone of Marcella's voice left no doubt that her annoyance with me was now as big as it had ever been.

I straightened the dress on the rack, then walked down around the end of the counter. She stood aside to let me pass. Her face was blank.

"I'll only be a minute," I said.

"All right."

I went into the back, swearing under my breath. Whoever was on that phone was going to get a balling out he or she would never forget. I hoped the caller was a male—Andrew, for instance, or even Fred—because the sound of a female voice asking for me would be enough to make Marcella angry with me for a week.

I snatched up the receiver. "Hello," I said briskly.

"Penny?"

I closed my eyes. Of all the goddamn people in the world to call . . .

"Who's this?" I said, trying to sound casual in case Marcella was listening.

"This is Bernice." She paused, as if uncertain of herself. "Did I interrupt anything?"

"Yes," I said. "I was busy up front in the shop."

"Oh, I'm sorry. It's after six o'clock. I thought you'd be knocking off by now."

"We usually stay open until around nine." I stressed the word *we* for Marcella's benefit.

"I can call back later if you prefer," said Bernice.

"I'll probably still be working," I said. "What's on your mind?"

"Well—" Again she paused, and I could picture that look of virginal embarrassment crossing her face. "I was only wondering if I was going to see you."

"Tonight, you mean?"

"Yes, that's right."

"No," I said, "I'll be busy." It hurt like hell to turn her down, but my prime concern at the moment was to pacify Marcella.

"Then—maybe tomorrow night?"

"I don't know," I said. "It depends."

"Penny?"

"What?"

"Are you mad at me?"

I ground my teeth together. I was in a pretty fix. If I said the wrong thing, I might turn Bernice away from me, and that would undo all the fine work I'd accomplished the evening before. On the other hand, the right words for Bernice would be the wrong words for Marcella; if I so much as made my voice the least bit friendly, Marcella would leech onto that clue and drive me crazy with her questions.

"No," I said, trying to sound noncommittal and affectionate at the same time. "Like I said, I'm just busy."

"Oh. I wondered. You sounded so cold."

Damn you, I thought, will you let it *go?* "I have a lot of work to do," I said aloud, feeling like a broken record.

"All right. When will I hear from you, Penny? Will you call me?"

"Sure," I said. "Maybe tomorrow. Or the next day. We'll see."

She was silent a moment. "I hope I didn't do anything to make you angry, Penny."

"Don't worry about it," I said. "Everything's fine."

"Okay. See you soon, then?"

"Right."

"Goodbye, Penny."

Her voice was so wistful that I almost blew the whole scene by answering in kind. The soft, sensuous longing in her words was unmistakable, and the sound of it pierced into the soft stuff beneath my belly.

I was barely able to control myself as I said, "Goodbye, Bernice."

She hung up. After a second, so did I.

I turned, feeling pretty proud of my will power, and discovered Marcella standing in the doorway, just as I expected she would be. My self-congratulation lasted only an instant.

"Bernice," said Marcella.

A chill went through me. "What?"

"Goodbye, Bernice. That's what you said. Bernice—she's the new girl at Pinocchio's, the one we talked about."

Damnation, I thought. I had tightroped all through that lousy conversation, only to fall off the wire an inch short of the platform.

"Yes," I said evenly. "That's the one."

"I thought you said she was a little clown. I thought you told me you didn't care for her."

My mind was racing desperately. "You heard me right," I said. "She's a real zero."

Marcella's mouth did something that was not quite a smile. "Then why is she calling you?"

I got a sudden inspiration. "She wants a discount," I said.

"She what?"

"I told her I worked in the shop here. She wants to buy her clothes from us at a discount." It sounded pretty thin even to me, but it was the best I could do.

"You're not telling me the truth, Penny."

I tried to look hurt. "Well, if that's what you want to believe, I can't do anything about it."

Marcella came a few steps forward. "You're having an affair with that girl, aren't you, Penny?"

Oddly enough, the anger was gone from her question, but I was too angry myself to wonder about that. "You're dreaming, Marcella."

"I don't think so," she said. "This has happened before, after all. I know the signs by now, Penny."

I felt my lips pulling back from my teeth. I had never been so close to telling Marcella exactly what I thought of her. A rage was building up inside me that I wouldn't be able to control much longer.

"You think you know everything," I said angrily.

"Penny, where you're concerned, I *have* to know everything." Her eyes looked moist for some reason. "You're terribly important to me."

"That's great," I said. "But so what? If you want to worry about me, that's your concern, not mine. You're not my goddamn *keeper*. I live my life the way I see fit, and if it doesn't please you—why, you can just go to hell for yourself. You follow me?"

"It *is* true," she said. "You—and that girl. Oh, Penny."

"Oh, *crap*," I yelled. "I don't need you to judge me. Not you, or anybody in the world."

"Penny! Please, honey, you don't understand—"

"Don't understand *what*? Don't understand that you're a suspicious old gossip? That you won't be satisfied until you have me in a cage, like a pet canary? That just because you pay my way, you think you own me? I understand all that *perfectly.*"

"Honey—" She was coming toward me, her arms held out. The moisture in her eyes threatened to turn into tears at any moment. "Don't call me names like that. I only want what's best for you. You're being so unfair."

"No, damn it, *you're* the one who's being unfair. I have my own life to lead, Marcella. I wasn't born just to jump through hoops for you. If I feel like having a little fling on the side, it's none of your cruddy business."

"Yes, it *is*, Penny," she cried. "I *love* you."

I sucked in a very deep breath, then dropped what I thought would be a real bombshell. "But I don't love *you*, Marcella. If you want to know the truth, I don't ever *care* for you particularly. If you dropped dead tomorrow, I wouldn't shed a single tear."

Marcella was sobbing openly. "I know that," she said, her voice breaking. "I have eyes, I have a heart. I never tried to fool myself that you felt the same way about me that I felt about you."

"Horse-wind," I shouted. "You're full of it, Marcella. If you cared a damn about me, you'd let me *alone.*"

"I *can't,* Penny. I'm so afraid you'll get hurt—"

"Hurt? By what?" An odd sensation was developing in the pit of my stomach. I could almost swear it was fear, but that made no sense. What did I have to be afraid of?

"Yourself," Marcella said. "I have to protect you from yourself."

"What are you talking about?" My voice sounded suddenly much weaker to me. The edge of my anger was gone, and the cold feeling in my belly was growing. Something was happening to me, and I couldn't understand it.

"You'll get yourself in trouble, Penny, unless you have somebody to always look after you. It's—it's the way you *are. I want* to look after you, honey. Please don't turn me away. I *love* you . . ."

Her voice was receding. So was the room. So was I. The eerie sensation in my gut was spreading through me rapidly. My vision grew hazy as the feeling mounted into my brain. I tried to speak, but my tongue was suddenly thick. A concept ballooned in my head, but the harder I tried to give voice to it, the more impossible speech became. Things damned up inside my skull until the pressure was almost too much to bear.

Then I saw the red.

Things were red again. *I* was red. Like blood, like rage, like a nightmare of horror, red, red, *red.*

Marcella's face swam in a crimson fog in front of my eyes. Her cheeks were filthy with tears, her mouth was open, talking, pleading; a moistly working hole which seemed, in my red world, like a hideous, palpitating wound.

I had to do something, but I didn't know what, because *doing* was part of conscious thought, part of volition, and my mind was incapable of decision, or even thought.

And again, as it had so many times before, the redness reached a pitch of menace which threatened to destroy me, execute me for my inaction.

So I did something.

It came from my glands, whatever it was, and my body performed it without the awareness of my mind.

I hung momentarily on the brink of chaos. Then, the redness began to fade, and I was safe.

When I came to my senses, I was sitting on the floor with my back against the wall. My arms were screaming with pain. Across the room, Marcella sat huddled in a chair, her face buried in her hands, her body heaving with sobs.

I pushed myself to my feet, ignoring the agony in my arms.

"Marcella," I said.

She didn't look up. "What?"

"I'm leaving, Marcella. We're through."

She stiffened. "Penny," she said. "Penny—*no*—" Her face began to lift from her hands.

I turned and ran from the room. Behind me, Marcella's voice mounted the scale into hysteria.

"Penny, come back! You don't *understand.* You *need* me to look after you. Penny—you'll get *hurt*—for God's sake, *Penny*—"

Then I was through the door and off at a run down the winding Village streets.

9.

I STAYED THAT NIGHT AT JOYCE'S PAD.

Luckily, she didn't have any affairs going at the moment, so she could accommodate me. I guess my agitated condition was pretty obvious, because she didn't ask any questions, didn't even try to make a pass at me. She just fixed up a spot for me on the couch and stroked my brow until I fell asleep.

In the morning when I woke up, she had already gone to work. There was a note for me on the kitchen table.

Penny: (it said)

There's bacon and eggs in the fridge. Help yourself. I don't know what your problem is, but try not to let it throw you. Take it easy today and think it out. If you feel like staying with me for a while, you're welcome. If you want to cut out, you don't owe me a thing.

Joyce

She was certainly being damned nice about everything. For a moment, I felt kind of guilty about it. After all, I had never done anything for her to earn such treatment.

I thought it over and finally decided that her generosity was founded on the usual ulterior motive—she probably figured that if she treated me well enough during my hour of need, I would give her the business in bed to show her my appreciation.

Nobody ever gave anything away without the expectation of getting something more valuable in return. That's how the world was.

I dismissed Joyce from my mind and concentrated on what had happened, and what I'd done. Marcella and I had gotten into the biggest argument we'd ever had, but that wasn't really the important fact. As loud and nasty as our disagreement had been, I imagined that she would probably be waiting to take me back if I offered her the chance. I had singed my bridges a little, but I hadn't burned them.

Far more fascinating to me was that blank I had drawn in the midst of our set-to. I could remember it only vaguely; it was another of those crazy spells I suffered every once in a while, and I could never recall them very clearly. I did know, however, that this particular blackout had been a humdinger; whatever it was that happened to me during those spells had happened this time with a vengeance. My arms were still aching slightly from it.

But the blackout had made even bigger changes in my brain. Up to the point where I had passed out, I'd had no real intention of leaving Marcella. Afterwards, it had seemed like the only thing to do. Now why in hell was that?

And why, right at this moment, wasn't I worrying about the loss of my meal ticket, feeling sorry for myself because Marcella wouldn't be paying the bills anymore? Why wasn't I trying to think of some way to get back with her?

And why on earth was I feeling so relieved?

I thought and thought, and gradually I came to the conclusion that it had been something she'd said. She'd made a statement, and it had been—what? Frightening? Was that the emotion which had made me run away from her?

I couldn't really tell. After a while, I decided to stop trying. I had made my decision, even if I didn't understand the reasons for it, and now it was time for me to give some thought to where I was headed.

Not back to Marcella—that was for certain. I had some money in the bank, luckily; not a hell of a lot, but enough to keep me rolling for a few months in the style to which I was accustomed. It was too bad about all the pretty clothes I was losing, but in order to claim them I would have to face Marcella again, and they just weren't worth it to me.

I made up my mind. First on the agenda was a trip to the bank. Then I would have to find a furnished room somewhere, lay in some food and some inexpensive clothing. And then—

Then I would get in touch with Bernice. And this time, there wouldn't be anybody around to interfere with my plans.

I thought briefly of the future, wondered what I would do when my money ran out, then wiped the thought out of my mind. Who gave a damn about the future? The present was all that mattered.

And my present was a pretty little package named Bernice.

I got to Pinocchio's that evening around ten-thirty.

Bernice spotted me instantly, and she looked so pathetically happy to see me that I nearly laughed in her face. I told her everything was all right, in answer to her questions, and explained that I had been curt with her over the phone because Marcella and I were in the middle of a fight. Of course, I didn't tell her what we had been fighting about, but

I did say that I was no longer either living with or employed by Marcella Lewis.

"I'm so sorry," she said when I'd finished. "You and Marcella were very close friends, weren't you?"

"Not all that close," I said. "Anyway, I think things will be better this way. With an apartment of my own, I'll be able to devote more time to my personal interests."

"Have you found a place yet?"

"Yes. Not very far from here, either. It's a cozy little pad. You'll like it."

"I will?" She looked puzzled.

"Of course. I thought maybe you'd drop in when you finished work tonight."

"Oh, Penny—" Her face glowed.

"I owe you some lessons, don't I?"

I sent her back to her chores. She kept glancing at me as she went from table to table, and it really tickled me to see the expression she was wearing. She acted as if I were simply too good to be real. For that matter, maybe I was.

Andrew didn't seem to be anywhere around, but I didn't much feel like talking to him anyway. I just sat, smoked, drank coffee and killed time until it was almost eleven. I thought of Joyce. I really should have given her a call to thank her for her hospitality, but I didn't feel like it. I thought of Marcella. What was the old butch doing now? Had she been looking for me? Was she all alone in the back of her cruddy shop, pining for my lily-white body, or was she out making it with somebody new? Whichever way it was, it made no difference to me.

I felt good. There was a smell of freedom in the air. All my life I had been dependent on one person or another—my parents, Marcella—but those ties were all cut now, and I was on my own. There might be trouble ahead, but I had the feeling that blond, little Bernice would make all the trouble worthwhile.

At eleven on the dot, she went into the back and changed her clothes. I was waiting by the door when she came up front a few minutes later. She linked her arm through mine, and we headed away from Pinocchio's toward my apartment.

I thought suddenly of Mark, her boyfriend, and wondered what the hell had ever happened to him. Bernice hadn't mentioned him once during our conversation. She acted as if he didn't exist. Could they have broken up? I found it hard to believe, but it was a possibility. Bernice was a good student, and at the rate she was going she'd be a graduate lesbian in no time at all.

My pad was located in a shabby walk-up on the third floor. The corridors smelled of urine and there was a lot of scattered garbage in the halls. I could tell Bernice was less than enchanted by what she saw. I hurried her up the stairs and got her into my apartment before she could get really turned off.

I had three rooms—a studio-type living room, a kitchen and a bedroom. According to the landlady, the layout had belonged to an artist up until the previous week. But he had been a pretty disturbed cat, and one night had painted himself out of existence by drinking a quart of denatured alcohol.

The pad he'd left behind was a knockout. The furniture belonged to the landlady, of course, but great things had been done with it—new paint and varnish on all the exposed wood, delicate shades for all the lamps, crazy paintings hung everywhere there was space on the walls. The apartment was neat, livable and striking as hell.

Bernice drank it in, and the disgust over the condition of the halls left her features.

"What a pretty apartment," she said, peering around like a little girl at the zoo. "I've never seen anything quite like it. Did you do all this yourself, Penny?"

"Sure," I said. "And it took a while, too."

"I'll bet it did." She shook her head in admiration. "You're so clever."

"You haven't seen anything yet, Bernice. Here—let me take your sweater."

In addition to the light sweater, she was dressed in a pale green shift, simple and sleeveless, which showed off the lovely lines of her body in subtle folds and hollowings of the material. She was wearing stockings for a change, and flats of the same shade as her dress. I had all I could do to keep my hands off her as I helped slip the sweater from her shoulders. She looked as inviting as a tall, cold drink on a hot day, although *tall* and *cold* were not very appropriate adjectives where Bernice was concerned.

I herded her over to the couch, sat her down, then went into the kitchen to whip up a pair of drinks.

Things were going beautifully. In spite of my troubles with Marcella, I hadn't lost any ground with Bernice. All the work I'd put into her was paying off in spades. And now it looked as if I were about to collect the reward of my efforts. I had her alone, finally, in an apartment of my own where no one could observe or disturb us. If all went well—and there was no reason for me to think it wouldn't—tonight would be *the* night.

I picked up the drinks, tried to hold them steadily enough to keep the ice from clinking, and went back into the living room.

Bernice was sitting on the couch with her legs stretched out in front of her. She had kicked off her shoes. It was a small thing, but it made me tremble. Her little feet were somehow just as beautiful as the rest of her, and seeing them made me remember her breasts and how they had felt in my hands.

"Here we go," I said as calmly as I could. "Drink up, and then we'll start working on your lessons."

She smiled, reached forward and took the drink out of my hand.

There was a knock at the door.

I practically had to bite my tongue to keep from cursing aloud. Of all the rotten times for somebody to be at my door, this took the cake. The atmosphere of intimacy which had been building in the room was shattered completely by the sound of that knock. Bernice's eyes came out of their dream and into the present.

"There's somebody at the door," she said.

"I know." I set my drink down on the coffee table.

"Aren't you going to answer it?"

"Just a minute," I said. "I'm thinking."

And so I was. Who in God's name could be out there? I had settled all my business with the landlady earlier that day, and I didn't know another soul in the building. None of my Village friends knew where I was, and that included Marcella. Of course, it was possible she had talked to Andrew about me and had somehow discovered the location of my new apartment. It would be just like her to come around and plead at my door.

The knock sounded again.

Well, what was I supposed to do? If I opened the door and had a scene with Marcella, I would probably ruin my chances with Bernice. On the other hand, I couldn't very well pretend there was no one out there; that would look pretty strange to Bernice, and might do just as much harm.

I had no choice. There was nothing for me to do but answer the door.

I crossed the room, feeling Bernice's puzzled gaze on my back. I plotted out my course of action quickly. If it were Marcella out there, I would get out into the hall before she and Bernice could see each other. I would close the door of the apartment so Bernice couldn't hear anything.

Then I would throw Marcella down the stairs. And if that didn't kill her, I'd jump up and down on her until I'd stabbed her to death with my high heels.

It was a stupid little fantasy, but I amused myself with it as I opened the door.

Mark was standing there.

10.

I'M SURE MY FACE must have looked as slack and stupid as a moron's at that moment, but fortunately for my self-respect Mark didn't even favor me with a glance. He stared right past me, his eyes scanning the room quickly, until he spied Bernice.

He took a step forward.

I recovered my composure just enough to put a hand against his chest. "Whoa, there," I said. "Nobody invited you in."

"Bernice," he called. "It's Mark, baby."

Behind me, I heard Bernice give a little cry of surprise. "Mark," she said, "what are you doing here?"

"That's what I wanted to ask *you,*" he replied.

I jabbed his chest with my index finger. "Suppose *I* ask that question—what the devil do you want? State your business."

I had finally succeeded in attracting his attention. He tore his eyes from Bernice and looked down at me. I had remembered him as being pretty tall, but at that instant he looked massive as a mountain. Before he even opened his mouth, I knew trouble was coming.

"Stand aside," he said. He spoke very softly, and that surprised me. I got the strange impression that he didn't want Bernice to hear him.

"This is my apartment," I said, fighting back the sense of doom which was invading my guts. "I only let in whom I please, and until I know why you're here—"

"They told me all about you," he said, in the same quiet way.

It took me the space of a heartbeat to absorb that. "*Who* told you *what* about me?" I meant the question to sound belligerent, but it didn't. My voice had dropped to his confidential level, and that took all the starch out of it.

He sighed heavily. "Those two young kids—the ones who tried to pick up Bernice the other night—I saw them again. I talked to them. They told me what you are."

I closed my eyes momentarily. God, but the world was filled with enemies. No matter how carefully you planned, no matter how painstakingly you covered your tracks, no matter how clever your disguise happened to be, there was always some bastard somewhere waiting to give you the shaft. Who in hell would have thought that those two snot-nosed punks could ever have had such a profound effect on my affairs?

I didn't have to ask Mark what they'd told him. I could practically imagine the conversation word for word. I had no answer for his accusation, so I sidestepped it.

"How did you find out where I lived?" I asked him.

"I followed you two," he said. "I was waiting a little ways down the street from that coffee house. I saw you and Bernice come out together." His face turned very ugly. "I know what you're planning, you crazy woman. I guess I've known it from the first time I met you and saw the way you looked at Bernice. Talking to those kids tonight was the clincher."

In back of me, Bernice piped up. "What's wrong, Mark? Are you coming in?"

"Let me pass," he said fiercely. "You've filled that girl's mind with enough poison."

He pushed me out of the way and stepped into the apartment. I left the door open and followed him across the room.

Bernice was on her feet.

"Why did you come here, Mark?"

"To get you," he said curtly. He grabbed her hand. "Come on."

She snatched her hand out of his abruptly. "Oh, no," she said. "Nothing doing. You're not taking me anywhere."

He turned to face her, and his huge body trembled with suppressed anger. "Look, Bernice—you don't understand what's going on. I'd prefer not to tell you. I'd like to spare you the knowledge of just how stupid you've been."

"Is that *so?*" Bernice crossed her arms under her breasts and cocked her head. "Well, maybe your idea of stupid and my idea are two different things. And maybe I'm not interested in your opinion of me, or of my intelligence." She pressed her lips together tightly for a moment. "When it comes to that, maybe I'm just not interested in *you* anymore."

"Cut it out, Bernice," he said. "Stop being an idiot."

All during this, I had been moving slowly toward them. I was careful to stay out of sight behind Mark. I still nursed the hope that something could be salvaged from this rotten turn of luck, and it would be better to let Mark forget my existence entirely and concentrate on Bernice. I kept my mouth shut and my ears open.

"I told you how I felt on the phone the other day," Bernice said. "Until you're ready to apologize for the nasty things you said the night I met Penny, I won't have anything to do with you."

Her statement hit me right between the eyes. I hadn't been reading her as well as I thought. She and Mark had been estranged since that first night at the bar, and I'd never even caught a hint of it.

"I'll apologize," he said, "but only after you've come away from here. I'm not kidding around, Bernice. This is more important than you know."

"*I'm* not kidding around, either, Mark. I know just how important it is. That's why I'm staying here."

"God *damn* it," he yelled. "In another minute, I'm going to grab you by the hair and *drag* you out of here."

"Sure," Bernice yelled back. "Why not? You're such a big, strong, hairy male. Why not show your superiority? Be a cave man—you practically are anyway. Punch me in the nose, why don't you?"

"Stop being a prima donna and do what I tell you, Bernice. It's for your own good."

"Oh, of course. Everything's *always* for my own good. That's what my mother used to say, and my teachers in school, and my friends. Well, I'll tell you something, Mark— nobody decides my own good but *me*. I'm responsible for myself. And not *you* or *anybody* is going to run my life for me. Is that clear, Mark?"

I felt like cheering. She was chewing him out expertly, and she looked so cocky and self-possessed standing there that I wanted to kiss her. I glanced at Mark and saw that her words had hit him where he lived. His big square shoulders slumped a bit and he passed a hand helplessly across his brow.

My sense of triumph faded. This was the critical moment. If he gave up now, turned and walked through the door in defeat, the victory would be mine. But if he stood his ground, if he were mad enough to spill what he had learned about me, then I would be the loser. And I had always been a poor loser, even when the stakes weren't as high as they were now.

I waited, my heart lurching in my left breast, wondering which way he was going to jump. I didn't have to wait long.

"All right," he said finally, straightening his spine. He stared directly at Bernice, and I could imagine the expression on his face by seeing the expression on her own.

This was it.

"Do you remember those two young punks who tried to pick you up the night you met Penny?" He said my name as if it were a dirty word. From his viewpoint, I suppose it was.

"Certainly," Bernice answered coldly. "You do a very good imitation of them, by the way. You're acting no better than they—"

He cut her off with a wave of his hand. "Stop babbling, and listen to what I have to say. You can insult me later."

"Very well," she said. "But make it quick."

"I saw those guys again tonight. I was waiting for you outside your coffee shop."

"You were waiting—" Her eyes went wide, then narrowed in anger. "You have some damned nerve, Mark

Hughes. I *told* you I didn't want to see you again. The very idea of having you *spying* on me."

"Shut up and hear me out, you silly little—" He bit off whatever he was going to say, but he might as well not have bothered. The tone of his voice was enough.

Bernice's pretty face turned to rock. She compressed her lips and said nothing as he went on.

"I've been worried about you, baby," he said, in a more conciliatory voice. "That's the only reason I 'spied' on you, to use your word. That night you met Penny and the three of us went to the bar, I sensed there was something wrong, but I couldn't put my finger on it. The way Penny acted toward you—well, it just wasn't *right*, that's all. I thought and thought about it, but I just wasn't able to figure out what was bothering me."

He dug his fingers through his hair in an agitated gesture.

I felt the way Marie Antoinette must have felt, with her head in the guillotine, listening to the whistle of the falling blade.

"So tonight," he went on, "I came down to the Village to see you, maybe talk to you, try to find out something about this woman you'd taken up with. I was there just a little while when I saw her go inside Pinocchio's, and I figured she was probably going to see you."

"I'm sure the F.B.I. could use a man with your talents," said Bernice icily.

He ignored her interruption. "While I was waiting, I saw those two guys coming down the street in my direction, and I remembered the fight you'd had with them and the way Penny had helped you out. I wondered if they would know anything about her. So I asked them."

"Tell me," said Bernice. "Did you punch them? Or do you do that only to girls?"

He was having trouble keeping his anger bottled. "They didn't want to talk at first. They were afraid of me, I guess. But as soon as I explained to them what I wanted, they told me the whole story."

He stopped and drew in a breath for the finishing stroke.

I couldn't stand it. My inaction was becoming too much to bear. I had to do something, anything, to cut him off.

I moved forward quickly and grabbed his arm. "That's enough," I said.

"Keep out of this." His words fell like stones into the room.

"I'm not going to stand around and let you tell this girl lies about me right in my own apartment, pal. Who the hell do you think you are, anyway?"

He whirled on me, his fists balled. "I'm Bernice's *friend,*" he yelled. "I *love* this girl, and I'll be damned if I'll let some cruddy *lesbian* ruin her."

Lesbian. The cat was out of the bag at last. I couldn't bring myself to look at Bernice.

"Shut your filthy mouth, you *bastard.*" I showed him my teeth. "You've got no right to call me names."

"You're *sick,*" he said. "You're out of your mind. I'm sorry for you, but I can't do anything about it. The only thing I *can* do is make sure you don't infect Bernice with the same rotten disease. I'm taking her away from you—right now."

"The hell you are," I said. "She decides that for herself. She's not your property, mister."

"Maybe not, but I'll be damned if I'll ever let her be *yours.*"

His face was twisted with anger. I glanced at his hands, which were still formed into tense fists. If I wasn't careful, I might just push him far enough to earn a clout in the head, and a shot from a man his size would be one to remember.

And then, suddenly, I had it. The idea sprang full-blown into my mind—the perfect way out of this, the ideal method of recovering Bernice, of undoing all the harm he had wrought. It was magnificently simple. It involved a little personal sacrifice, but I had already come this far and the prize was worth a bit of extra effort.

My lips curled back in a sneer. "Big man," I said mockingly. "Can't convince himself he's a male unless he's got a woman under his thumb. I know your type, Buster—women aren't *people* to guys like you; they're just pieces of flesh designed to make you feel good."

"Damn you," he said. His fists swung heavily at his sides.

"Sure," I went on, still sneering. "A man's not a real man unless he can dominate a female or two. Your kind likes to make us *crawl*, get down on our knees and kiss your feet and acknowledge your male superiority. You call *me* sick? Mister, you're sicker than I'll *ever* be."

His face was growing very red. "You bitch," he said, hissing it between his teeth.

"*That's* the way," I shouted. "Call me dirty names. Tell lies about me. Make up filthy stories, because that's all a mind like yours can think about. Prove what a hero you are, and then you can go down to the local gin mill and tell the boys how you make your women crawl, and you can all have a great big laugh over that. And afterwards, maybe you could

all go to the local whorehouse and pay some skinny little slut
to build up your ego even more—"

That did it.

As usual in moments of stress, my time-sense slowed
up, giving me a leisurely opportunity to watch what was happening.

I had time enough to realize I was going to get hurt and
brace myself for it.

But there was also time for me to think: *Now you've torn it,
you big clod. From this moment on, she'll belong to me.*

His fist hung in the air, as big as the harvest moon. I
watched with deep satisfaction as it hurtled toward my face. I
saw the whiteness of his knuckles, saw the crisp hair on the
back of his hand, last of all saw the fine network of lines
which crisscrossed his fingers.

Then he nailed me.

The impact was terrific. I felt my head snap backward on
my fleck. The patchy ceiling swam above me, and I struggled
to maintain my balance, as well as my consciousness. I knew
there would be pain shortly, but in that instant I was feeling
nothing but triumph.

I stayed on my feet. The muscles of my face were numb,
but somehow I managed to keep that sneer intact. My voice
didn't sound as if it belonged to me.

"You're no better than a goddamn *queer,*" I said.

He hit me again. This time, his blow was even more
fierce; and this time I felt it. A bomb of pain went off in my
skull. I felt a warmth on my upper lip and realized my nose
must be bleeding. How beautiful, I thought; the sight of
blood would be the final touch.

My knees were buckling, my eyes were hazing over, my ears were ringing with a thousand unanswered telephones. But I didn't care. The last thing I saw was Bernice moving forward, her fingernails locked into claws, drawing a neat set of parallel red stripes down one of Mark's cheeks.

The last thing I heard was her voice screaming at him:

"You *beast*—you rotten *animal*—I hate you, I *hate* you! I never want to *see* you again—*never!*"

Within the privacy of my own thoughts, I roared with laughter.

Then the goddamn floor tilted up and slammed against the back of my head.

11.

I HUNG IN DARKNESS for quite some time, but it was a warm and satisfying sort of darkness and I enjoyed it. There was no trace of red in it anywhere, no menace, no pressure, nothing I couldn't understand. My mind was shut down, and if there were room in it for any thought it was the glowing realization that I had won.

Eventually, the darkness passed, and I swam slowly toward the light. Through half-lidded eyes, I could see a pale blue expanse above me, and it took me several seconds to figure out where I was. Then I felt starchy folds of sheet against my back and realized I was in the bedroom. The artist who'd had the apartment before me had painted the bedroom ceiling sky-blue, and now, as I awakened to that restful color, I knew what he'd had in mind.

A warm golden sun moved suddenly into that peaceful sky. It had a face, the way suns do in children's books, but the face wasn't smiling. In spite of the warmth it radiated, that sun looked as sad as a winter moon.

It spoke.

"Penny," it said softly.

"Hi, Bernice." I tried to smile, but it hurt my mouth.

Her features twisted in sympathy. "Oh, you poor darling. What did he *do* to you?" She had a cloth in her hand and wiped my mouth with it tenderly.

"I'm all right," I said. "Nothing's broken."

"I was so *scared*—I didn't know what to do, whether I should call a doctor, or the police, or what."

"I don't need any help, Bernice," I said quickly. "I'll be okay—as long as I have you to take care of me."

She allowed herself to smile. "I'm sorry," she said.

"Sorry? What for?"

"It was my fault. He was my boyfriend. If I'd had any sense, I would have made sure he stayed away from you."

"Oh, come on," I said. "You're not responsible for what he does, any more than he's responsible for you. We all make mistakes, Bernice. Just be glad you found out in time what he was."

"Am I *ever,*" she said. "I never realized what a brute a man could be."

She was quoting directly from the little book I carried around in my head, the one called: *How To Talk Like A Lesbian Without Really Trying.* It was music to my ears.

A thought hit me, and I frowned. "What happened to him?" I asked. "Is he around anywhere?"

"No, he's gone. I threw him out. I gave him some pretty bad scratches. He'd better have somebody look after them."

"He just left? Didn't he try to take you with him?"

"Oh, he tried, all right. He raved and yelled all sorts of crazy stuff. If even half of it were true, you'd have to be the Queen of Hell." She wrinkled her nose.

The Queen of Hell—I liked the sound of that. Mentally, I tipped my hat to Mark for having coined such an appealing title.

"Do you think he'll be back?" I asked her.

"No," she said positively. "I told him off. We're through."

"*You* feel that way," I said. "But are you sure *he* does?"

She twisted her mouth. "Well . . . maybe not. But I don't give a damn how he feels about it. After what he did to you tonight, I just don't want to ever see him again."

"Help me sit up, Bernice."

She got an arm under my back and lifted me to a sitting position. When I moved my face, I could feel dried blood all over my lips. There was a rotten taste in my mouth, probably also blood. I felt rotten all over—physically, that is. Mentally, I was happy as a lark.

"You're all dirty," said Bernice. "We have to get you washed up."

"I guess I could use a bath," I said. I slung my legs off the end of the bed and tried to stand. I was halfway up before I realized that my legs wouldn't hold me. Apparently, I was still plenty woozy from the beating I'd taken.

I sat down heavily on the bed.

"Penny—what's the matter? Are you hurt?" She grabbed my arm.

"Dizzy," I said. "I'll be all right in a minute."

"Is there anything I can do for you?"

A sudden inspiration struck me. This seemed to be my day for inspirations. "Yes," I said. "I think a good hot bath would probably cure what ails me. Would you give me a hand into the bathroom?"

She got to her feet and helped me up gently. "Take it easy now," she said. "Don't strain yourself. Just lean on me."

Leaning on Bernice was something I didn't mind at all.

She supported me across the bedroom and into the bathroom. The short walk revived me completely. The dizziness cleared, and my limbs came back under my control. But I didn't let Bernice know about my recovery. In the bathroom, I continued to play the part of the poor injured female, the victim of filthy male brutality.

She sat me down on the rim of the tub and started the water running into it. She tested the temperature as carefully as if she were drawing a bath for an infant. She straightened up and smiled at me.

"What else can I do, Penny?" She seemed to be enjoying her Florence Nightingale role, and that suited me fine.

"I'm all stiff," I said sorrowfully. "Could you help me with my clothes?"

She hesitated briefly, and in that hesitation I could see the germ of my final triumph. There was nothing in the simple concept of helping me undress to give her pause—unless she was attaching some personal importance to it. A woman doesn't get excited or embarrassed over removing another woman's clothing, doesn't react to the sight of a female in the bathtub.

A woman doesn't—but a lesbian does.

I leaned forward a bit. "Get that back zipper," I said.

Her fingers fumbled for the tab, found it and drew it down. I rounded my shoulders and plucked the bodice of the sleeveless dress down to my waist.

I grabbed her arm and pulled myself erect. She slipped the dress down my waist to the floor. She had apparently removed my shoes when she arranged me on the bed, so now the only garments remaining between me and nudity were my brassiere and panties.

She looked at my near-naked body briefly, then turned and tested the tub temperature again. Her face was growing flushed, and the steam rising from that tub had nothing to do with it. I think I was getting a bit flushed myself.

I showed her my back. "Would you undo my bra now?" I asked.

This time, her pause seemed to last forever. When her fingers finally touched the fastener, they had it open in one eager snap. The cups clung to my sweat-moistened skin. I faced her again, gave the loosened straps a slight tug, and felt the bra fall away.

My breasts were free and quite naked. I glanced down at them and saw that the tips were already pebbled with excitement. Bernice also saw that and, though I don't think she recognized the significance of it, the sight obviously fascinated her.

"Bernice," I said softly. "Now my panties."

No pause this time. Her fingers hooked into the elastic waistband and whipped the lacy panties down to my ankles in one quick motion. I felt her fingers working on my calves as she lifted each of my legs in turn free of the crumpled undergarment.

Right then, I knew I had her. And it was a terrific temptation to take her, get from her all that my efforts had earned. But I really needed that bath. Sex with Bernice would be fun under any conditions, but it would be a hell of a lot more satisfying when I felt clean.

So, instead of making a pass at her, I climbed into the tub and settled down into the warm water.

"This won't take long," I said. "I'm feeling better already."

She nodded. It had been several minutes since her eyes had looked into my face. "Is there anything else I can do?" she asked.

"No—I don't think so." I reached for the soap.

"Wouldn't you—" She didn't quite get it out.

"What, Bernice?"

"Wouldn't you like me to—" She bogged down again, licked her lips, then raised her eyes to my face—"to wash you?" she asked, very quietly.

I sat unmoving in the tub for a long time, long minute, staring into her eyes, seeing the freshly stoked furnace of excitement blazing there, feeling the deep, sweet coilings of my own excitement.

Silently, I lifted my hand and gave her the soap. Then I stretched myself out as far as the tub would permit. The only parts of me above the surface were my head, my knees and the very tips of my breasts.

I closed my eyes and waited for her to begin.

She began.

At first, her touch was stiff, uncertain, without warmth; but gradually her hands forgot the idea of cleaning my flesh and concentrated on caressing it. I could feel each of her moving fingers as separate little pressures, and it seemed to me that they left prints all over me, tiny circles of sensation to mark the places where they had been.

My flesh began to tingle.

She never did get around to using the soap, but that was all right. The heat of the water rinsed most of the discomfort from my body, the touch of her hands did the rest. Several times, she passed her palms across my face in a soothing caress which wiped away all the blood and left a warm anticipation in their wake.

I felt my breasts captured in her hands. She held them tenderly, as if afraid she would crush them. The tips bloomed against her palms. Then her hands left my bust and were sweeping beneath the surface of the water, down my sides, along my hips and flanks, the delicate fingertips trailing across the white globes of my buttocks.

To this day, I have no idea what happened between the bathroom and the bedroom. I don't recall getting out of the tub. I don't know what I said to Bernice or what she said to me. I don't remember which of us dried me off. I have no recollection of whether I removed Bernice's clothes in the bathroom, or later on in the bedroom.

When I finally returned to my senses, it was only to lose them again. I was standing beside the bed. Before me, spread out like a banquet of flesh, was Bernice, rosy, rounded and naked.

Her body was everything I'd hoped it would be and more. The ripe mounds of her breasts lolled slightly on her rib cage, but the swell of them remained as clean and perfect as ever. The taut berries of the tips rose in naked invitation.

Her smooth belly rounded when she inhaled, hollowed as she exhaled. Her thighs looked sleek as marble and at the same time soft as cloud. There was a small vein in her creamy throat which beat with the rhythm of her heart.

I slid onto the bed next to her. My hands touched her belly, then came seeking upward toward a breast.

"Penny."

My hands stopped. "What, Bernice?"

"Mark," she said. "He called you a lesbian."

I said nothing.

"Penny—isn't a lesbian a girl who likes other girls?"

"Yes," I said.

"Does a lesbian hate men?"

"Yes."

"Then she can't have sex with a man. Is that right?"

"Yes."

"So—" I could feel her body breathing beneath my palm—"if she wants to have sex, she must have it with another woman. Is that correct?"

"Yes."

"And if she wants to love somebody—wants somebody to love her—" The breathing became more rapid—"then that somebody must also be a woman. Is that what a lesbian is?"

"Yes," I said.

She shifted her shoulders, inched her body down the sheets, and suddenly a warm, soft breast had been delivered into my hand.

"Then I'm a lesbian," she said simply.

We fell together and spent the rest of the night proving it.

12.

SHE WAS THE FIRST THING I SAW the next morning.

The pale light of dawn shone through the bedroom window, making her flesh look like pearl. We had slept together, numb and sated, without any covering through the night, and now I was awakening to find her lovely body still there beside me, still almost too beautiful for my mind to grasp, still yearning for the love of my mouth and my hands, even in sleep.

I couldn't quite believe she was real. I cupped my hand over the top of one thigh, wanting to convince myself of her solidity, needing to know that this sweet creature was made of real flesh and not the mists of my own fantasies.

I touched her, and suddenly she was awake. Our eyes met, locked, and I could see the memory of all that had passed between us glowing in her gaze.

For a single frightening moment, I wondered if she were going to accept what she had become. It was a big step in her life; it meant throwing over everything she had ever believed, ever been taught, and learning to think and act in an entirely new way. Did she have the guts to follow through? Or was this to be the morning after, the awful awakening when a person is forced to run rather than face the guilts of pleasure?

Her body remained still for only an instant longer. Then she rolled herself hungrily up against me. Our lips met, our tongues writhed, our hands rediscovered all the secrets of our flesh.

When we woke again, it was long past noon.

That evening, Bernice and I went to Pinocchio's and talked Andrew into giving her the night off. He wasn't very fond of the idea, but he agreed anyway. Being short of help annoyed him, but he was so fascinated by the sight of Bernice and me together that he wouldn't have refused us anything.

His eyes silently asked the question. My eyes answered it. His mouth crooked in that fey smile of his, and I knew we had won his everlasting approval. Bernice didn't notice it, but he blew us a kiss as we left. Andrew was like that. He loved his own kind, and few things pleased him more than a new recruit to the club.

We rode uptown to Bernice's apartment. It was a dreary little pad, as characterless and drab as a hotel room. For some reason, it reminded me of Mark, and I think Bernice felt the same association. We were both glad when we had packed her things together and had gotten out of there.

Back at my place, we unpacked her meager belongings, divided the closet and bureau between us, and settled down in the living room for a long talk. Oddly enough, our conversation never once touched on the subject of lesbianism but confined itself to the homely little details of our life together.

We discussed money. I told Bernice how long my nest egg could be expected to last. I lied about the actual total, figuring that a reserve fund might come in handy in case Bernice and I didn't last. We decided that she should keep her job at Pinocchio's for the time being. We could live comfortably if I matched her salary each week from my savings; and I promised her that when my money ran out I would see about getting a job.

Naturally, that was a promise I had no intention of keeping. Except for my years at the dress shop, I had never held a job—you couldn't exactly call my relationship with Marcella *employment*—and I wasn't about to start working now, not even for Bernice. When the time came, I would think of something.

We talked about the apartment. It wasn't really large enough, but with the two of us sharing everything equally we could make do with it for a while, anyway. If it didn't work out, we could always scout up a larger pad.

Presuming we lasted together, of course. I kept that thought to myself.

We talked and talked, planning things out until we were both satisfied with the arrangement. Bernice was very matter-of-fact about the whole thing; a bit too much so, I couldn't help thinking. But there was no time for her calm acceptance of this new life to make any real impression on me, because suddenly it was bedtime, and we both knew it.

We undressed quickly and slid in side by side under the sheets.

It was midnight when I switched off the bedroom lamp.

It was three A.M. when we finally fell asleep.

That was how it started.

And it wasn't long before I could see a pattern forming. The days passed, flowing one into the other, and there was a comforting sameness to it all. We'd awaken together late in the morning, caress and kiss each other, sometimes make love. Then we'd go to the kitchen and eat a healthy breakfast. After that, we'd shower, occasionally together, and that quite often led to another session of love-making. When that was done, we'd dress and busy ourselves around the apartment until it was time for Bernice to report for work. Pinocchio's was only five minutes away, which meant we could be together right up to two fifty-five in the afternoon. We frequently used the time for more sex, and Bernice would leave for the coffee shop with her face flushed, her eyes bright, her hair in disarray.

From three o'clock on, I spent my hours alone, thinking.

There was a great deal to think about. It's a characteristic of the human breed that no one ever really plans beyond the attainment of a goal. Every ounce of mental effort is poured into the process of getting where you want to be, and no thought at all is given to the question of what you'll do when you get there. People are like that—they can see the top of the mountain clearly, but they seldom have brains enough to imagine the valley on the other side.

I was suffering from this common ailment. I had worked to win Bernice against great odds. The battle had cost me a great deal. Now it was over, I was the victor, Bernice was mine. So what next?

Would we just continue to live together indefinitely? That was a pleasing prospect at the moment, but I doubted if it would still please me after a year or so. Bernice was a delight in every way, and she was still learning. But her charms would have to pall on me sooner or later, if only because they would become so familiar. Our relationship could endure for a while, perhaps even a long while. But not indefinitely.

I wondered if Bernice realized that fact. Probably not, I decided. After all, this was her first lesbian affair, and she was young and silly enough to think that an agreement of mutual physical pleasure between two females could be as sound as a marriage. Some day soon, I would have to apprise her of the facts of life. If she kept that foolish notion fixed firmly enough in her head, we would be in for a sticky scene when the time came to call it quits.

I would have to begin asserting myself pretty soon. Thus far, Bernice and I were coasting along on a more-or-less equal basis and, while that was enjoyable, I knew myself well enough to know I wouldn't stay satisfied with it. Sharing Bernice's body was a delight, but *dominating* her would be an ecstasy.

In the broad scheme of things, I could see only one flaw, one single imponderable. And that was Bernice herself.

She had changed since that first night we spent in each other's arms. Of course, a certain amount of change was to be expected. She'd gone into that session as a virgin, and she'd emerged as an accomplished lesbian. Her physical virginity was still intact, but mentally she'd been thoroughly raped.

And yet, that wasn't the source of the oddness I felt in her. When we talked together, I could sense a certain withdrawal in her manner, as if her mind were shrinking away from me. Nothing of this showed in her speech or her manner, but I knew it was there just the same. It bothered me.

Had that first time in my arms actually been the turning point for her? I had thought so, but I was no longer so sure. Maybe she *hadn't* faced the consequences of her decision. Maybe she had run from it, closed her mind to it, refused to consider the course she had chosen. Without all my careful preparation, I was sure she would have fled screaming the moment I first touched her body; but had my groundwork been sufficient? Had I touched her mind as well as her flesh?

The more I thought on it, the more convinced I became that Bernice was suffering from a disease known as *guilt*. She didn't seem to know it herself, but the signs were there for me to see. Guilt is a nasty illness for anyone, but for a fledgling lesbian it's fatal.

So, in opposition to my natural instincts, I had to postpone my gradual domination of her. If any of her mind was still rebelling at the idea of a lesbian relationship, then the seed of disaster was planted between us. One false move from me, one hint of the fact that our intimacies were founded on physical gratification rather than love, and Bernice would run like a rabbit. As irritating as it was, I was forced to nurse her along, treat her tenderly, behave like a simpering lover, handle her as if she were the most precious thing in the world to me, instead of just a round little blonde who fed my base hungers.

For a person like me, it was damned hard to maintain such a pose. But I did it. I had to satisfy Bernice's guilt feelings before I could own her completely. Once I had made her mind accept it, the sky would be the limit.

One evening, Bernice and I met at Pinocchio's just before she finished work, and we caught an Ingmar Bergman flick at a local theatre. Art movies usually bore me, but I liked this one pretty well because there was a rape in it. They did the sequence with a great deal of restraint and symbolism, but no one could possibly miss what was happening to that poor girl up there, what the man was doing to her.

All through the film, I kept identifying with that man and stroking Bernice's breasts whenever I got the chance.

It was very late when we left the theatre. Bernice acted tired, but I was wide-awake and raring to go. The movie had really put me in the mood, and I was busy thinking of ways to prevent Bernice from falling asleep on me when we got home when I realized somebody was following us.

I don't know what tipped me off. Maybe it was the sound of the footsteps on the pavement. Maybe it was a shadow, a stirring, a rustle of clothing. Maybe it was some kind of telepathy. All at once, my mind was brought up short by the knowledge that there was someone behind us.

I didn't even have to look to know who it was. But I did, anyway; surreptitiously, as Bernice and I turned a corner.

Marcella.

She was about half a block behind, trailing along as clumsily and steadily as a bloodhound. She made no effort to catch up to us, but she kept us in sight, all the way back to the apartment.

It ruined my mood. For an hour after locking the door, I waited for the sound of her feet on the stairs, for her knock on the door. Nothing happened.

Bernice, as I expected, undressed, showered and went straight to bed. I did the same. All through the night, my brain swam with dreams of Marcella. If I could have gotten to her at that moment, I think I would have killed her.

The next day, Bernice was even more withdrawn than usual. I didn't do a thing to help her out of it. I was in a pretty withdrawn state myself. I thought of nothing but Marcella. Why had she followed us? Had that been the first time, or had she trailed us before? Would it be the *last* time? What the hell did the woman *want?*

Bernice left for work at two forty-five. I don't think I even said goodbye to her.

At three-thirty, I had an attack.

It hit me all at once, with no warning. One moment, I was sitting on the couch quietly; the next, my brain was flooded with red, blotting out reality, extinguishing thought, filling me with that perilous crimson pressure I knew so well. My mind reeled under the burden of it, and a deeply hidden part of me screamed *danger, danger—*

I had to *do* something—the thing I always did when these fits were upon me, whatever that was. I was consumed by heat and redness, and it would destroy me if I didn't give it release.

I did something.

I came to much later, sprawled on the couch, my body soaked with sweat. The muscles of my arms were shrieking with pain.

I had done something. I had performed the old ritual of catharsis, purged myself the way I always did, the way I never understood.

But it hadn't been the same. Some vital element had been missing. And though the hideous red pressure had faded, it had not been satisfied, not this time. It was still in me somewhere, lurking, waiting to grow again.

For the first time in my life, I began to feel genuinely frightened.

13.

ONCE I KNEW ENOUGH TO LOOK, I began to see Marcella everywhere.

Whenever Bernice and I went out, sooner or later I would spot her behind us. She tagged along even when I was out by myself, always keeping the same distance between us, walking when I walked, stopping when I stopped, vanishing into the shadows when I tried to get a good look at her.

It made me so angry I could hardly think straight. Several times with Bernice, I came within a hair of challenging Marcella, running back to her and clawing her eyes out. But I held myself in check. I didn't want Bernice to see that.

One afternoon when Bernice left for work, I went to the living room window and looked down into the street. I saw Bernice come out of the building and head off toward Pinocchio's. An instant later, I spotted Marcella standing in a doorway on the opposite side of the street.

She didn't make any move to follow Bernice. She hardly gave the girl a glance. Her face was lifted, her eyes were fixed on my window.

I jumped back out of view, trembling in every limb. I couldn't bring myself to look again until night had fallen.

Then, with the lights in the apartment turned off, I edged over to the window and stared down.

She was still there, still gazing patiently upward, standing in that doorway as if she were willing to wait for me forever.

The unsatisfied core of redness flared up in my brain—not into a full-scale fit, but just far enough to flood me with anger. I left the apartment and charged down the stairs. This time, I had no Bernice to worry about, and I intended to run across that street, grab Marcella and whale the living tar out of her. I was as mad at that point as I had ever been, outside of the crazy rages that sometimes tormented me when those fits struck.

I burst from my building at top speed and raced over to Marcella's doorway.

She wasn't there.

I couldn't believe it. I had seen her standing there from my window, and it had taken me less than a minute to get down to the street. Where could she have gone in such a brief time? *Why* had she left the doorway? Was it just coincidence, or had she somehow known I was coming down to confront her?

That was nonsense, of course. She didn't have X-ray eyes; she couldn't see into my apartment, watch my movements, know my plans in advance.

Could she?

I stood there for a few minutes, calming myself down, glancing covertly around to see if I was being watched. When I caught my breath, I began walking. I didn't want to return to the apartment—not quite yet, at any rate. For some weird reason, I associated the pad now with Marcella. Sitting up there, even in the dark, and knowing her eyes were on my window—

The thought made me shudder. I felt safer on the open street.

But safer from *what?* Why in hell was I getting into such a sweat over Marcella's attention? All right, so she was following me around; a stray dog might do the same thing, and for the same reasons, and that wouldn't bother me at all. The old dyke was probably lonely for me and tagged after me every chance she got so she could look at me, stare hungrily at my body, remember how it had been with us before the balloon went up. Actually, the idea of that was pretty laughable.

I didn't feel like laughing.

I walked for hours. My feet carried me west to Washington Square, then north on Eighth Street, across Broadway, out of the Village entirely and over to the shabbiness of the Bowery. I was approached by several drunks whining for handouts, but I cursed them away from me.

Every so often, I glanced back over my shoulder.

Marcella was following, always following, with unhurried pace, demanding nothing, threatening nothing—just following.

It was nearly one o'clock when I finally got back to my apartment. I was weary in every bone. I felt drained of anger. As I started into the building, I caught a flash of movement out of the tail of my eye. I turned to look.

The street was empty.

But she was *there,* goddamn her—I could feel her presence, feel the brush of her mind against my own. She was there, she was watching, she was thinking about me. And I knew that when I went into the building, she would station herself again in that doorway across the street—and watch.

I climbed the stairs slowly to the third floor. It wasn't until I reached the landing that I realized Bernice was probably already home. I would have preferred to be alone at that point, but there was nothing I could do about that.

I opened the door and went in. Bernice was sitting on the couch. She was smoking a cigarette, and that surprised me. She didn't care very much for tobacco and usually settled for a few puffs of mine after we finished a session in bed. I had never seen her smoke a cigarette of her own before.

"Hi, Bernice," I said. I crossed the room and sat beside her.

She didn't look at me. "Hello, Penny."

Her voice sounded strained. Something was wrong. All of a sudden, my fatigue left me, and I was completely alert.

"Are you all right?" I asked her.

"Yes." She paused and picked a shred of tobacco from the tip of her tongue. "Where were you?"

"I went for a walk. Felt like getting some air."

She nodded. "How come you didn't stop by Pinocchio's?"

For God's sake, I thought, was the silly kid insulted because I'd gone somewhere without her?

"I wanted to be outside," I said. "The walls were pressing in on me. I needed some sky. You know how it is."

"Yes—I know how it is." She repeated the sentence as if it were a terribly profound thought.

Was this *it*? I wondered. Was this the crisis point I had been anticipating? Was she beginning to wake up to reality, see herself and me for what we really were?

I examined her face, and what I saw in it did nothing to reassure me.

"Bernice? What's the matter?"

"I don't know," she said.

"Don't you feel well?"

"I don't know how I feel. That's the trouble."

"Tell me about it." One of her hands was lying on the couch cushion. I put my own hand over it gently. She pulled it away.

"I can't tell you what it is, Penny, because I don't understand it myself."

"Tell me how you feel," I said. "Maybe I can help you figure it out."

She puffed inexpertly on her cigarette, then leaned forward and stabbed it out in an ash tray.

"Penny?"

"What?"

"Do you love me?"

I could feel my face go slack. "Love you? Well—sure. Certainly, I love you."

"I don't mean just *like* me, Penny, I mean *love*—real love."

"Bernice, I told you I loved you, and I meant it. Now stop talking in circles and tell me what's troubling you."

"That first night we spent together," she said slowly. "I asked you what it was like to be a lesbian."

"I remember, Bernice."

"And you explained to me that two women could have sex together, enjoy each other's bodies almost the way a man and a woman might. You told me lesbians could live together and never feel the need for a man because they would have everything they required, companionship, sex—and love."

I didn't remember saying all that, but I nodded anyway. "That's true, Bernice."

"Do you *really* love me, Penny?"

"Why do you doubt it, Bernice?"

Her brow furrowed in concentration. "I don't know. It's just a feeling I get sometimes. We're living here together, and we have pleasure, we share everything, but—"

"But what?"

Her eyes came up and held mine. "Penny? Can one woman really love another woman? Can that happen?"

"Of course, Bernice. It *has* happened. To us."

"Is it *right*, Penny?"

I didn't answer her right away. I was thinking furiously. This was the turning point. She had dragged out all her guilts and was examining them, and the ugliness was too much for her to absorb. If I didn't find a way to ease her through this crisis, I would lose her—lose her without ever having really owned her, without ever having bent her to my will, made her my slave. I couldn't let that happen. I would go crazy if it did.

"Bernice?"

"Yes, Penny?"

"Will you wait here for me?"

She blinked. "Where are you going?"

"There's something I have to do. I won't be long. And when I come back, you'll see how much I love you."

"Will I?"

"Yes, Bernice. I promise you."

I left her sitting there, grabbed my purse and went down to the street. I didn't bother to look for Marcella. I had more important things to think about.

It wasn't easy to find a florist open, but Village stores keep peculiar hours and I connected on the third try. I bought the most expensive corsage he had—a white orchid with a pale gold center.

Next, I found a gin mill where the bartender knew me, and I talked him into selling me a quart of champagne. It cost a pretty penny, but it was worth it.

Last of all, I hit a card shop and bought the biggest, sloppiest I-Love-You greeting card I could find. It had lace all around the edges of it. It cost two dollars. I inscribed it, bought some gift paper, wrapped the corsage and the champagne, and hurried back to the apartment.

It was a big act, of course, but it might help do the trick. Bernice knew how short the money was, and when she saw how much I had spent to cheer her up she would probably pull out of her doldrums. I'd fill her with champagne and flattery, play the part of the mooning lover, convince her I was everything she wanted me to be.

And when I was sure the mood was right, I would take her to bed and treat her to the most tender and thrilling intimacies any girl had ever received.

If I did it right, if I played the part to the hilt, everything would be fine. She would belong to me from tonight on, and I could do with her any damned thing I pleased.

I climbed the stairs and let myself into the apartment. The living room was empty. I set the gifts and the card down on the coffee table, arranged them artistically, then turned off all but one of the lamps so the room's lighting would be properly cozy. That done, I went into the kitchen and got two glasses down from the shelf over the sink. I rinsed them quickly, dried them and carried them back out to the coffee table.

Then I went into the bedroom. The bed was empty.

I stood frozen for several moments, not allowing myself to think. I turned and went to the bathroom. The door was open, the light was out. I flipped the switch anyway.

There was no one in the bathroom.

Nor was there anyone in the bedroom, or the living room, or the kitchen.

There weren't any other rooms.

Bernice was gone.

I ran back to the living room in a frenzy, snatched up the bottle of champagne and shattered it against the wall.

14.

I HAD BEEN AN IDIOT, and now I was paying the price.

Leaving Bernice at that crucial moment was the worst thing I could have done. She had been alone too long that evening anyway; she's had too much time to think things out, to feel the pressures of her guilts. She had been right on the edge when I came home. If I had stayed with her, I might have been able to swing her over.

But I hadn't stayed. I'd gone out instead to buy her gifts.

And while I was out, the guilt had driven Bernice past the point of no return.

She was gone.

I stood in that living room and howled every foul gutter word I knew at the top of my lungs. I must have shocked hell out of the neighbors, because doors were open and people were staring at me as I left the apartment and pounded down the steps. I didn't give a goddamn about any of them. The anger in me was too big and too red. If they'd tried to stop me, I think I would have killed them.

But nobody tried to stop me.

I hit the street at a dead run but brought myself up short when I remembered Marcella. I don't know what made me think of her at that moment. I looked all around me, peering into her favorite doorway, examining every patch of shadow, every possible concealment.

I didn't see her. I didn't *feel* her, either. The subtle pressure of her attention was gone from the air. Wherever she was, her eyes were not watching me.

The hell with Marcella. The hell with everybody.

I started running again.

Bernice had to be somewhere in the vicinity. She couldn't have gone very far in the short time I'd been away. I was determined to find her, drag her back to the apartment and make her pay for ducking out on me. No more tenderness, no more words of love, no more holding back—if I couldn't keep the stupid broad, then I would at least have the full use of her once. I would strip her, take her, make her violently, show my mastery over her.

Nothing less than that could satisfy me.

I tried Pinocchio's first.

Andrew nearly dropped his teeth when he saw the state I was in. He kept trying to soothe me, quiet me down, glancing past me nervously at his customers.

"Please, dear," he said, "you're shouting."

"I'll *stop* shouting if you'll just answer my goddamn question. Where is she? Is she here?"

"Is *who* here, darling?"

"Bernice, you silly fag—who the hell else would I be asking about?"

He looked miffed. "No, she isn't here. She left work hours ago."

"Did she say anything about where she was going?"

"Yes—she said she was going straight home. To *you*, darling."

"Thanks a lot," I said sourly.

As I left the place, I heard Andrew say, "Really dear, she's *your* responsibility now."

I went to the bar where she and I and Mark had stopped that first night. I checked all the booths, even looked in the ladies' room, then collared the bartender, described Bernice vividly, made a commotion until he would answer me.

She hadn't been there.

I headed out into the street again, half crazy with anger and frustration. I began hitting every bar and coffee house I could find. People on the street fell over themselves getting out of my way, and I felt them staring at me. I must have made quite a spectacle of myself. Thinking back on it, I wonder why nobody called the police and had me taken away.

All things considered, being thrown in jail would probably have been the best thing that could have happened to me.

But nobody tried to stop me. I was free to run from one end of the goddamn Village to the other, looking everywhere, stopping total strangers for information, dashing around until my lungs were ready to burst, until my eyes felt ready to fall out of my head.

No one knew where she was. No one had seen her.

She was just plain *gone*.

I stopped at last on the steps of an apartment building and sat down. My body was so clenched up and trembling that I could hardly remain upright, even in a sitting position. The redness inside me—the crimson residue left by that unsatisfied spell I'd had—was growing more intense. I felt rage and fear all mixed together in my head, and the combination was more potent than either emotion. If something didn't happen soon to relieve me, I would burst.

A hand touched my shoulder.

I leaped to my feet with a yell and whirled to see who it was.

"Penny! Take it *easy,* for God's sake. What's the matter with you?"

It was Joyce. I realized that the steps I'd been sitting on led up to her building. I hadn't recognized it until that instant.

"Bernice," I said. My throat was hoarse.

"Bernice? You mean that little blonde you've been shacking up with? The one who works at Pinocchio's?"

I swallowed hard and nodded.

"What about her?"

"Where is she?" I cried. "I've been looking all over the Village, and I can't find her anywhere."

"Well, I'll be damned," Joyce said. "I thought it looked kind of funny, but I figured you had to know about it."

"Know about *what?*" I grabbed the neckline of her blouse, pulling her toward me. "You mean, you've seen her?"

"Sure," she said. "Just an hour ago, approximately."

"Where was this?"

"Christopher Street. Near that cruddy antique shop. You know the one."

"Did you talk to her?"

"Uh-uh," Joyce said.

"Well, did you see where she was heading?" Do you have any idea where she might be?"

A peculiar expression crossed Joyce's face. "I don't really know what the destination was, but I *do* think I know where you could find them."

My fingers dug into the material of her blouse. "Them?" I repeated. "Was she with somebody?"

"Marcella," Joyce said.

I flung her away from me, snarling like an animal. She sprawled back across the steps, and I heard her cry out in pain. I didn't stop to apologize. I didn't stop for anything. I rocketed off down the street, heading as fast as I could toward the dress shop.

Inside my head, the crimson pressure was building furiously.

The shop was dark, but I could see a light glowing in the back room through the glass of the display window. I tried the doorknob. It turned, and I went in.

I slammed the door loudly behind me and ran toward that light, my fists clenched in a frenzy. I knew what I was going to see even before I got back there, but that didn't mean I was prepared for it.

Marcella.

She was sitting on the bed with a pillow propped behind her back. She was totally naked. In one hand, she held a burning cigarette. In her other hand, she held a sweetly rounded breast.

The breast belonged to Bernice. She was sitting beside Marcella and was just as nude. Her nipple was ripe with excitement in Marcella's fingers, but her face seemed completely blank. Her eyes were wide open, but dead.

"You rotten *bitch!*" I shouted. "What the hell do you think you're doing?"

Marcella smiled. I had never seen her smile quite that way before. It was cold, humorless and somehow very cruel.

"What does it *look* like I'm doing?" she said tightly. "I'm having some fun with this little girl."

"Get your hand off her," I hissed through my teeth. "She belongs to *me.*"

"Not anymore, sweetie." The smile grew. "She's *mine* now. Aren't you, dear?" She jiggled Bernice's breast in her hand. Bernice didn't say a word. She didn't even seem aware of my presence.

"Now, *listen*—" I began, but Marcella cut me off. She released Bernice's flesh, threw her cigarette into an ash tray and climbed off the bed. She crossed the room toward me, her full breasts dancing with the motion, stopped, spread her feet and put her hands on her hips.

"You've *had* it with this girl," she said. "You ought to know by now how the game is played. You grab what you can get, hold onto it as long as possible, get every kick available. But you can't make it last forever. Sooner or later, it's got to end, and you lose your playmate to somebody new. And when that happens, there's nothing to do but go looking for fresh meat somewhere." She paused, and the smile vanished from her face. "It's about time you learned what it's like to lose something you wanted. You're not really grown up until you've felt a pain like that. I know all about it, you see."

My arms and legs were quivering. I couldn't think of a thing to say. Over Marcella's shoulder, I could see Bernice still sitting on the bed, looking straight ahead at nothing in particular, like a propped-up corpse. I didn't have the wit to wonder what was wrong with her.

"Get out of here," Marcella said. "This is a private party."

I jumped at her, my hands reaching for her throat. She blocked me easily with her arms and belted me open-handed across the face. Her blow was nearly as strong as Mark's had been.

I fell against the door jamb, breathing raggedly.

Marcella's eyes glittered. "Go away, little girl," she said quietly. "*You're* the loser this time."

I turned away and stumbled through to the front of the store. The taste of defeat was like poison in my mouth.

15.

I WANDERED MINDLESSLY.

The streets were crowded, but I paid no attention to anyone. I let the mobs carry me to and fro like a bit of garbage in a river current. It was Saturday night, but I didn't know that. I was garbage, and what does garbage know?

Nothing.

Every so often, the crowd would carry me into a bar, and I'd have a drink—not because I wanted one, but because it was the thing to do. I don't know how many gin mills I hit or how many shots I poured into myself, but it must have been quite a load.

Gradually, the alcohol began thawing out my mind. My brain felt like a ball of ice melting, dripping little meaningless thoughts. After a time, those thoughts started running together, forming a little puddle of awareness in my brain.

I was mad.

I was so goddamned mad I could hardly bear the intensity of the emotion. I wanted to strike out around me, hurt somebody, hurt everybody, hurt the world for what it had done to me. I wanted to feel somebody's throat in my hands, somebody's blood warming my fingers.

I was mad enough to kill.

It scared me, and I drank some more, trying to drown it. If I drank enough, I reasoned, I would render myself completely numb, incapable of anger. Maybe I would be able to pass out. I hoped so. Oblivion would be pretty welcome.

But it didn't work out that way. Every drink I took only fed my rage, like small glasses of gasoline thrown on a fire. The fire grew and grew, and the phoenix of my anger thrived in the center of it.

I reached the point at last where alcohol could no longer do anything for me. My anger was as huge as it could get without destroying my mind and, as long as it remained there unsatisfied, no amount of drinking could relieve me.

I had to do something.

Strange that that particular image should cross my mind. The concept of *doing something* was connected with those red fits of mine, those eerie spells of unconsciousness which seemed to take so much out of me—

I didn't bother to follow the thought. The workings of my brain had ceased to interest me. At the moment, I was suffering from a deep and terrible hunger, and I had to feed it before I could allow myself to think again.

Fate.

That was the bastard who had done me in. Things had been going my way for so many years that I'd forgotten that bad luck and good luck are opposite sides of the same coin. I was so used to turning up *heads* that *tails* had ceased to exist for me.

But Fate hadn't forgotten. Fate had kept his eye on me, adding up all the good luck I'd been granted, making a mark opposite my every stroke of fortune. For each good, there must be a bad, or else things don't balance out.

So Fate waited and waited until the time was ripe. And now I had to pay for it all in one stroke.

Revenge.

It was the only answer. I had been hurt. I had to therefore hurt in return. It was simple and symmetrical, and Fate, who liked to make things balance, would no doubt approve.

The question was, *who?*

I thought of going back to the dress shop and taking it out on Bernice and Marcella, but that wouldn't work. I could remember well the way Marcella had spoken to me, the feeling of her hand exploding against my cheek. Everything had changed, Marcella included. There was a power in her now, an iron determination that was completely new to me. I had no idea where she had gotten it, but I knew I would be powerless to fight it.

I needed a victim—a natural-born weakling who could suffer at my hands. A male would do, but I would prefer a female: some soft, trembling little bunny who would cower before my anger, shrink up into a nice compact target . . .

A girl like Bernice.

If I took up a station outside the dress shop and waited long enough, she would have to come out eventually. In terms of balance and poetic justice, giving her the business would be the most appropriate move of all.

But I rejected the idea. If I knew Marcella, she would keep her new playmate in the sack all night, and I didn't relish standing on the street that long. Besides, Bernice wasn't really responsible for what had happened. I was certain of that. She never would have gone to Marcella on her own hook. Marcella had come to her, gone up to the apartment while I was out making a fool of myself, buying flowers and champagne, charmed Bernice into submission as I was intending to do, and stolen her away from me.

It was Marcella. It had always been Marcella. I knew I could never rest until I had *destroyed* Marcella.

Time enough for that when I could think clearly. Right now, I had to find an outlet for the red sickness inside me. I needed a *victim*.

I went looking for one.

I found *five* of them.

They were all sitting on a bench on the west edge of Washington Square. They were young, unsure of themselves, but determined not to let the world know it. I recognized the type the instant I saw them.

Five young girls—their eyes bold in their smooth faces, their growing breasts even bolder in their tight blouses, their rounded buttocks barely contained by the tight slacks they wore, their toes spread and uncomfortable in the sandals they thought they had to wear.

Perfect.

They saw me coming. The five faces examined me from head to toe. They struggled to show no expression, but an awakening of interest was plainly there.

"Hi, girls," I said. "Looking for some kicks?"

"What's that to you?" The girl on the end seemed to be the spokesman for the group. She was a saucy little thing, with midnight-black hair and a round face. In a few years, she would turn into a slut, but right now her youth was still working for her.

"Well," I said, smiling, "when I see five cute chicks like you sitting around doing nothing on a Saturday night, naturally I get interested."

"You a cop?" she asked.

I laughed. "No."

"A social worker," she said disgustedly. "I know your type."

"Wrong again," I said.

She narrowed her eyes. "Then what the hell are you?"

I paused a moment for effect. "A dyke," I said.

Her eyes went wide. "A—you're kidding."

"Why would I kid about a thing like that?"

"You're a butch? Honest to God?"

"What makes you doubt it?"

The kid leaned forward, fascinated. "You don't look like one. I always thought lessies were square and ugly-looking—like William Bendix, or something."

I chuckled. "You might be surprised how many good-looking girls prefer to get their kicks with other girls."

"Maybe I would," she said.

"You ever try it?" I asked her.

"What, jazzing dyke-style? Hell, no."

"Why not?"

"Because . . ." She stopped and looked puzzled. "No reason, I guess. I just never met anybody I'd do it with."

"How about the rest of you gals?" I asked, scanning the row of upturned faces. "Any of you ever make it the lessie way?"

"Them?" The black-haired girl snorted. "Not likely. They only do what I do. I run the pack here."

I nodded. "You look like a leader," I said.

She puffed out her chest proudly, like a young boy. The small mounds of her breasts strained against her blouse. "That's me," she said.

"All right, what do you say you do some leading right now?"

Her face went suspicious again. "How do you mean?"

"There's a bar not too far from here that caters to a very special kind of customer. Usually they don't admit anybody as young as you girls, but I think I can get you in."

"So it's a bar," she said. "So what?"

"It's a gay bar," I answered.

"Hey—you mean one of them places where all the pansies hang out?"

"No pansies," I said. "The only male in the whole place is the bartender. The rest—well, you figure out for yourself what the rest are like."

"A dyke bar," the girl said, half to herself. "I never knew they had places like that."

"How about it, leader? You game?"

She grinned suddenly. "It sounds like a gas."

"What about the rest of the crew?"

"We're with you, sister. Let's go get some kicks."

"Follow me," I said.

The place I had in mind was called Casey's, which was the nickname of the old butch who ran it. I had been snowing the girls when I told them I could pull strings to get them in. I didn't know any of Casey's regulars; and besides, that place would let in anybody old enough to walk, as long as she was female. Once inside, you were on your own.

I had heard that you could order aphrodisiacs right across the bar, just like ordering a drink. I didn't know if that was true or not. But I did know that there were several small rooms available in the back for the use of those customers who felt the urge, had no other place to go, and were willing to meet Casey's price.

Of course, I could have saved money by taking the girls up to my apartment, but I didn't think that would work out so well. In order to get them loosened up enough for what I had in mind, I needed the wild and hellish atmosphere of a bar in full swing. In a place such as Casey's, anything went.

I came in with all five of them trailing behind me and grouped them in a knot near the end of the bar. I bought a round of drinks and watched with amusement as they choked them down, pretending they were used to the taste of liquor. They were a tough little crowd, but it wouldn't be long before I'd taken all the toughness out of them.

I could hardly wait.

I left them for a minute on some excuse or other, asked one of the dykes where Casey was, and was directed to the old butch herself. She was brisk and businesslike, and her eyes made no secret of the fact that they were gobbling me up.

The legend was right—you could buy aphrodisiacs at the bar. The chemical they used, Casey assured me, was completely tasteless in liquor.

I ordered five of them.

I also lined up a room large enough to hold us all. It cost a wad, but I didn't care.

I went back to the bar, told the girls to drink up, and gave the bartender the high sign. The round of doctored drinks appeared as if by magic.

Power.

I was really feeling it. These stupid girls were going to regret this night as long as they lived. I would see to that. Once the drinks started working on them, they wouldn't be able to resist me. I'd have them. I'd *ruin* them. I'd filthy them in a way that would never clean off.

I often wonder what happened to those girls. They finished those drinks, so they must have felt the intended effect. I doubt if they got out of that bar with their little hides intact. There were plenty of beady-eyed dykes in the place besides me to take care of them.

But I wasn't there long enough to find out.

I had just put my hand on the black-haired girl's soft rump when the door of Casey's opened, and Marcella stepped in.

She walked over to me and put her arm around my waist. Her touch was very gentle.

"Penny," she said. "Let's go home."

16.

THE BED IN THE BACK OF THE STORE WAS EMPTY. Bernice was gone without a trace. But I myself was too far gone to even notice it.

For me, it was over. Perhaps Marcella had appeared at an appropriate psychological moment. Perhaps my anger had simply grown too intense to support itself and had burned out. I can't explain what happened to me.

But when Marcella walked into Casey's and touched me, I had no power left to resist her. I just let her bring me back to the old place, loosen my clothing, arrange my tired limbs on the familiar bed, as if nothing had ever come between us.

I slept for a while. I don't recall dreaming. The oblivion which had eluded me all evening came at last to claim me, and all the hurts and rages were soothed by the comforting darkness.

When I awoke, it was morning. Marcella was sitting on the bed next to me, wearing a light robe.

The events of the night before came rushing back into my head painfully, and I had to cup my face in my hands in order to sort them all out.

"She's gone," Marcella said.

"Where?" I lifted my head and looked at her. She was smiling, the old smile I remembered so well.

"I don't know. To California, I imagine."

"California?"

"She told me all about her boyfriend, his job, her acting—the works. She went back to him."

"And—and you let her go?"

"Certainly. I didn't want her."

"Marcella—I can't follow you. If you didn't want her, why in hell did you steal her from me?"

"I didn't," she said. "I stole you from *her*. I wanted you back again, Penny. It was the only way I could think to do it."

"Is that why you trailed me everywhere I went?"

"Yes. I was waiting for an opening. Sooner or later, I knew I would find a way to get you back."

I shook my head. I was having trouble absorbing what she was saying.

"By the way," Marcella went on, "she wasn't a lesbian."

"I know that," I said. "I thought I could make her one, but it didn't work."

"You had her pretty mixed up, you know."

"So what?" I twisted my mouth. "Who cares about her?"

"Nothing," said Marcella. "It doesn't make any difference, anyway. I straightened her out."

"How?"

"The way you saw me doing," she replied. "I was just getting started when you burst in on us." Her face softened. "I'm sorry about the way I treated you, Penny. I had to do that for Bernice's sake. I wanted her to see what it was really like to be a lesbian, how painful it could be to lose a partner."

I didn't say anything.

"After you'd left," Marcella continued, "I really went to work on her. I made her every way I knew how—and I know quite a few ways." She laughed. "It was disgusting."

"Disgusting?"

"Sure. That was the whole idea. Instead of treating her gently, making certain she had a good time, I did everything I could to make her feel *filthy*. I groveled on her like a pig. I tell you, it got so bad at the end that I stopped enjoying it myself."

"You drove her away," I said.

"That's right. All she needed was the right kind of treatment to snap her out of it. Once she'd seen the underside of lesbian life, she was cured. She left here screaming, calling for her boyfriend. I hope she found him. I hope he's sensible enough to nurse her along until she gets over what happened." Marcella shrugged. "But that's no longer any concern of ours, is it?"

"Why?" I asked.

"Why what, honey?"

"Why did you do it, Marcella?"

"I told you. To get you back."

"That was no way to get me back. You must have known how mad I would be over what you'd done."

"Yes, I thought of that."

"Then what the hell were you trying to do? What did you think you were going to accomplish?"

She chewed her lip for a moment. "I was—I was trying to help you, Penny."

I snorted. "You call that help?"

"Protect you, then. Yes, that's the word. I wanted to protect you."

"From what?"

"From yourself."

A funny coldness was developing in the pit of my stomach. I tried to ignore it.

"You've said that before, Marcella—protect me from myself. What do you mean by that?"

She looked away. "It's better if we don't talk about it, honey."

"We *have* to talk about it," I said. "I'll go crazy if I don't find out what you're driving at. You make it sound as if you know some kind of big secret."

She didn't answer me.

"Marcella? What is it? What's the secret?"

"Penny . . ."

"All these years, you've put up with me, paid my way, stood back and done nothing while I played around on the side—what's the reason far that, Marcella? Why didn't you dump me ages ago?"

She spoke very softly. "Because I love you, Penny."

"That's crap," I said.

Her head snapped up. "It's *true!*" she said fiercely. "I loved you the first moment I ever laid eyes on you, and I've never stopped. Not even—"

I grabbed her arm. "Not even *when*, Marcella? For God's sake, *say* it. Tell me what you're talking about."

"It's—" Her face was filled with pain, "—your sickness, honey."

"My sickness? You mean, the fainting spells I get?"

"They aren't fainting spells," she said.

I couldn't stop myself from asking the question, even though I didn't want to hear the answer.

"What are they, Marcella?"

"You—" She licked her lips. "When those fits hit you, honey, you turn into somebody else."

"I do *what?*"

"Your whole personality changes, Penny. You become a different person. For as long as the spell lasts, you're a total stranger."

I closed my eyes. All at once, I could see the redness again. It hung there behind my eyelids; a small spot of crimson.

It was growing.

"What kind of person do I become, Marcella?" I asked without opening my eyes.

Several seconds ticked by before she answered. "Cruel," she said.

"What do you mean by *cruel?*"

"You—you want to hurt people. You need to inflict pain. It has something to do with sex, I think. You act as if you get intense pleasure out of hurting me."

"You."

"Yes, Penny," she said. "I'm always here. I always watch to see if it's going to happen. And when it does—I just let you do it to me."

"You let me *beat* you?" I was remembering the bruises I'd seen on Marcella's face, and how she'd always explained them away by saying she'd fallen or walked into something. I was also remembering the soreness in my arms that followed my blackouts—as if I had been using my muscles in some terribly strenuous fashion.

"I let you work it all off on me," Marcella said.

"Why?" I asked.

"Because if you did it to someone else—" She paused, and I heard her take in a deep breath. "They might put you away."

I didn't say a word.

"I really love you so much, Penny. I swear to God, I'd do *anything* to keep you safe. That's why I'm always so worried when you take up with somebody else. I'm afraid you'll have one of your fits, and hurt them, hurt them *badly*. And if that ever happened, they'd lock you up, Penny. And I'd lose you forever."

I said nothing. I was watching the red. It had grown from a small disc into a monstrous sphere. It almost filled my entire field of vision. In another moment, it would.

"You'll see, honey," Marcella said. Her voice was growing distant. "It'll be just like old times again. We'll settle down together, share our lives, make love, and I'll always be here to protect you, Penny. Please believe that. I'll never let them get you." Her voice cracked. "Penny, you're all I have in the *world.*"

I opened my eyes.

I couldn't see anything but the red.

"Penny," she said.

The pressure was building. The fire was burning in my skull. Everything was red, hideous red, dangerous red.

There was peril. I could sense it without being able to name it. The red could destroy me, flare up hotly enough to reduce me to ashes.

I had to *do* something.

I was off the bed in a single motion. Dimly, through the pulsating redness, I could see Marcella's face.

And beside it, I saw the faces of my mother and father.

The red was *hate*.

And I did something.

Much later, I lay in the bed beside Marcella, waiting for sleep to come. Her face was patched with bandages. Her left eye was swollen, her lips were puffy.

I had done quite a job on her.

I looked at her sleeping there, and suddenly I felt terribly tired.

Marcella, I thought, *in all the world, I have only one enemy, and that's you.*

You're the one who's going to destroy me some day—destroy me with that simple-minded love of yours. You're going to love me, and care for me, and take all that punishment from me without a whimper—and eventually, I'll kill you.

And then it will be too late, Marcella, too late for both of us.

Don't you see? If they'd gotten me in time, they might have been able to cure me. You're not taking care of me, Marcella—you're taking care of my disease.

It can't last forever, Marcella. Your love is going to kill us both.

I lay back with my hands behind my head.

What was the point of worrying about it? Marcella and I were already dead. Nothing was going to happen, no one was coming to save us, things weren't going to change. We were dead, and for a corpse there's no future but the worms.

I fell asleep at last, side by side with Marcella, in our red and empty tomb.

The End

About the Author

Jessie Dumont is the pseudonym of a well-known author who has published more than thirty novels during the past ten years. Born in Brooklyn and educated there, Jessie Dumont spent a number of years as a court reporter before joining the ranks of full-time freelance writers.

Also on Blackbird . . .

KEPT	Sheldon Lord
YOUNG AND INNOCENT	Edwin West
ELIZABETH TAYLOR	John B. Allan
SHABBY STREET	Orrie Hitt
BLOOD SUNRISE	Seth Edgarde

Check out our other great titles at:

BLACKBIRD BOOKS
www.bbirdbooks.com

Milton Keynes UK
Ingram Content Group UK Ltd.
UKHW040616240124
436603UK00004B/170

9 781610 530163